Trauma Town Dispatch

a novel

Suzann Kale

This is a work of fiction. All of the characters, organizations, and events portrayed in this novel are either products of the author's imagination or are used fictitiously.

Photo Credits:
      High Heeled Leg - ralwel/123RF.com
      Headset - karandaev/123RF.com
      Heartbeat - Rebellion Works/Shutterstock.com

ISBN: 9781079575033

For **Emilie**, JAMIE, *Michelle*, Megan, **Ian**, Aidan, **Maddie,** and Jesse. And for Melanie, Bobi, **Dawn**, Sandy, Michelle, Courtney, and PAT

Melissa P my amazing friend and editor. **Kip**, *precious beloved Jake,* Hollis and Greg. And

Mike

Love to Lisa and Dawn, Lynne, Joyce, Amanda, Annette, Denise, Laura, and Gudrun.

Love to Dad and Team New York/Connecticut!

Gratitude for having been a part of Pleasantville High School's class of '65. Love to Pris, Ellen, and Frank. And Dave Barry, my first boyfriend (was it 5th grade?) who I evidently forsaked for my horse Frosty.

Fuzzy shout-out to Lexie on the Rainbow Bridge. We miss you, puddytat.

Chapter 1

She was close to death, but not in a good way.

The night they brought Juliet into the emergency room, everything changed for Sabine.

Usually it was the person on the stretcher, being rushed in through the ambulance entry doors, whose life was catastrophically changed. But Juliet, even though she was completely unconscious, had it all together.

Sabine, on the other hand, was watching her mind race through a thriving repository of possible catastrophes.

Although she had seen Juliet at their condo over the past few years, getting the mail, passing her in the hall, they never spoke much. Juliet had a distance about her, and Sabine hated to get into people's faces. And now her neighbor was on a possible death bed, and they had never connected.

Occasionally Sabine had tried to make small talk in the hall, with things like "We hauled a dead body in from the park last night". But Juliet would just smile graciously and float into her apartment on a draft of Coco Mademoiselle.

What little Sabine did know about Juliet had mostly to do with Juliet being a Vietnam vet. Sabine felt that she and Juliet had a great deal in common, both of them being in healthcare. Juliet had been a nurse in the war. Sabine was a switchboard operator at Trummel Hospital. Juliet was gorgeous and aloof. Sabine always wanted to be gorgeous and aloof.

So that night, Juliet came into the hospital, unconscious, admitted through the emergency room. Sabine knew about it because there was a police scanner running continuously in the switchboard room where Sabine answered phones and dispatched ambulances.

"Unconscious person, female, Bravo level" came through the scanner and then Juliet's name came out of the printer. Sabine thought she heard the word "unresponsive."

Federal privacy laws prevented Sabine from ripping her headset off and running to the ER to see what was going on. Everyone from switchboard to surgeon had to sign a document swearing to keep patient information as private as a tomb. You hear something compelling on the police scanner, you catch a glimpse of a shocking diagnosis on a patient's chart, you hear someone screaming from a distant hall somewhere - you hold back any urge to connect or transfer information in any way. You might quietly call Security about the screaming. In an extreme situation, you might whisper to the switchboard operator next to you that Water Rescue was trying to recover a man who had been under Lake Trummel for forty minutes, but since the water was cold, might still be alive. But mostly you just lay low and kept working.

So Sabine quietly took her headset off, switched her phone over to Operator Glo's desk next to hers, and wandered upstairs to the ER for a coffee.

And there was Juliet, her cream satin nightgown dripping out from under the ambulance blanket as they wheeled her into an exam station. Her golden-blond hair was in a flawless updo that the EMTs were unable to mangle, and her diamond stud earrings made her look like Grace Kelly.

"Juliet!" Sabine whispered in her ear.

Lulu, the ER nurse, pulled Sabine into the exam station with Juliet, as she closed the curtain, leaving the EMTs in the hallway. "You know her, Sabine?"

"She's my neighbor," Sabine said. "Juliet Indigo. Is she ...?"

Lulu did the blood pressure and pulse checks. She checked the IV the EMTs had hooked up. "I mean,

her blood pressure's low, and I'll need to do some
tests. But no, she's not …". Lulu gave Sabine a look.

"Hello, people do die here," Sabine countered.

"Your friend is fine."

"I don't really know her."

"Damn," Juliet mumbled. Her eyes fluttered
open and her color blushed back to vitreous from pale.

Sabine bent over her. "Jesus, Juliet. What the
hell?"

"Help me sit up," Juliet whispered.

Lulu cranked the bed into the sitting position and
started in with her stethoscope. The blanket fell to
Juliet's waist. Her luxe satin robe was unwrinkled, her
makeup was flawless, and her red nail polish was
unchipped just as it always was when she got her mail.

Sabine looked at her. "So?"

Juliet turned a glazed *Last Year at Marienbad*
gaze on Sabine and Lulu. Sabine half expected her to
start speaking French, but Juliet was from Brooklyn,
like her. And now she was Sabine's neighbor at the
condo in Trummel, in the middle of nowhere, up along
the Hudson River, too far north to get into the City often
enough to stay sane.

"I don't know, Sabine," Juliet finally said. Even
sick, her voice was dusky and dense like the last sip
from a deep glass of burgundy. "I went down to get the
mail and then here I am. You know?"

"I get it, Juliet," Sabine reassured her with an over-exuberant half-laugh. "One minute you're walking down the street and the next minute you're regaining consciousness in the ER. Yes. Life as we know it."

Lulu looked out over the top of her glasses. "You're killing me, Sabine." She messed with Juliet's IV bag. "How do you feel, Juliet?"

Juliet refocused on Lulu. After a long pause she said slowly, in a hushed, late evening dinner voice, "I believe a psychological component has come undone."

Sabine felt a slight arrhythmia in her chest as she realized she kind of knew what Juliet was talking about. But Lulu was clinically on top of it.

"What came undone, Juliet?" Lulu prodded. "I mean did this component cause some discomfort somewhere?"

"Yes, there have been repercussions," Juliet explained. "Cause and effect, right?"

"Okay. Good," Lulu said. She took off her glasses and bent in close to make direct eye contact. "So let's think about repercussions. I'm talking about like something that hurts? An actual body part, like a stomach, perhaps, or a leg?"

At that point a team of ER nurses and techs thundered by the exam station as Operator Glo's voice heralded a new disaster through the hospital overhead paging system.

"Attention all personnel, Rapid Response Team to the main parking lot. Rapid Response Team to the main parking lot."

Sabine peeked out of the curtain.

Operator Glo, Sabine knew, always got a little manic when she got to make these overhead announcements, but like all the hospital operators, she held it back with practiced experience. In addition to working the switchboard and dispatching ambulances, operators at Trummel Hospital were the voices that paged doctors, announced codes to send teams running to resuscitate people, and called the Fire Department each time the kitchen dishwasher started smoking.

Though some hospital personnel such as social workers thought of the operators as lower down in the caste system, Sabine and Glo loved working in real time, sitting in Telecomm at the switchboard waiting to pounce on the next catastrophe, and being the connecting factor to all people, sick and healthy, saviors and savees. It was like holding a live wire in each hand and having your body connect the electricity between them. To announce an emergency hospital-wide, and say things like *helicopter en route* and *stat*, and to talk to the police dispatchers saying *nineteen hundred* instead of seven o'clock, were some of the many perks of working in the basement for not too much money and no ventilation.

The rapid response code that Operator Glo just called meant that Sabine had to get back to the switchboard at Telecomm quickly. Glo would need help with whatever was going on. Sabine took Juliet's hand to try to get her attention. "So Juliet, I have to get back to work. Lulu's going to figure out what's wrong with you."

"No, you're not understanding the situation," Juliet said. "I knocked something loose and I need to go home to put it back."

"What was knocked loose, Juliet?" asked Lulu, still eager to get a handle on her new patient.

"Oh." Juliet was sinking back into a faint again. "My wine glass." That was it. Her eyes fluttered closed. A small tear dripped down her cheek without running her eyeliner.

Lulu mumbled, "Oh lord, why is everyone who comes in here nuts."

"Cut her some slack, Lulu," Sabine said. "She was a nurse in Vietnam, for Godsake."

"We've all got our storylines," Lulu said.

"You've got to take Bill W off your Twitter," Sabine snapped.

"Bill W is my Go To Meeting guy."

"I know and that's wonderful. Call me at the switchboard if anything comes up."

Lulu saluted, and Sabine power-walked through the jittery fluorescent light in the twisted hallways, her straight brown hair streaming behind her. Dodging flying spit from a coughing phlebotomist, she caught a back elevator and went down two floors to the switchboard room in Telecomm.

"Where have you been?" Glo had a vein in her neck that was bulging, red, and pulsing. All the switchboard lines were blinking. She pushed a button and went back to her phone. "This is Operator Glo, how can I help you?"

As operators, Glo and Sabine were trained to keep their voices low and smooth when announcing some horror over the hospital overhead system. Keeping calm was supposed to aid in paging the right doctors to the right operating rooms, and the correct administrators to the correct command centers, all without frightening the patients or alarming the social workers.

Sabine rushed to her desk next to Glo, slammed her headset on lopsided wrecking her bangs, and picked up the next call. "This is Sabine, thank you for calling Trummel Hospital, how can I help you?"

"It's the Trummel Sun," a male voice barked. *"We heard there was a shooting. Who got shot?"*

"Um, shot? Hold just one moment please." Sabine looked at Glo next to her, but Glo was in a zone, knocking one call out after another, her hysteria expertly held in by her love of rising to the moment.

Sabine left the newspaper guy's line blinking, and took the next call in her queue. "This is the switchboard, Sabine speaking -"

"Sabine, it's Dr. Raj. I'm in the ER. Get the RT on call, bring her in stat." He hung up.

"Here we go." And Sabine dove into concentrated speed mode, which meant cutting back on all extraneous activities like breathing, so she could focus completely on finding a respiratory therapist. Her fingers flew over the keyboard as she typed in the RT's on-call beeper number.

The need for a respiratory therapist meant that whoever was having this medical emergency - whoever got shot? - was at least breathing. Or they weren't but they could be. You don't need an RT if there's no breathing going on. So that was a piece of information, a clue. This was what it was all about – gathering the information necessary for survival that no one wants you to have. "Glo, what's the deal?"

"I'm not sure." Glo tapped onto the next call. "This is Operator Glo, how can I help you?" She put her hand over her headset microphone and turned to Sabine. "I called a Rapid Response Code."

"I know, I heard it, I came running back here." She clicked her keyboard. "This is the switchboard, Sabine speaking -"

"Sabine, it's Victor. The police are here. They've put the hospital on lockdown. I need you to call a Code Purple."

Victor Brazil was the head of Trummel Hospital Security. He was blond and good looking, except for severe eye bags and a blanched, protein deficient complexion which everyone overlooked because he wore a uniform and there weren't all that many middle aged single men in Trummel.

"Yes, I'll call the code right away. What happened, Victor?" Sabine felt dizzy, which was a bit of a high, but when she remembered to breathe the dizziness went away. She quickly flashed on the half bottle of Merlot sitting on the counter by her fridge at home. She saw from her console that Victor was calling from the emergency room. "Did someone get shot? Are they okay?"

Victor hung up.

With patient information sacrosanct, you could actually go to jail for doing something wrong in the privacy department. As a result, and since everyone was always running around trying to keep people from stroking, choking, or having their hearts stop, there was no time to ponder the privacy rules when you had to convey information. Consequently people shared as little information as possible to as few departments as possible, in order to lessen their chances of breaking some rule. That translated to no one knowing what anyone else was doing.

"This is the switchboard, Sabine speaking."

"*It's Lulu. Dr. Raj says to call a Code White.*"

"Victor said Code Purple."

"*Fine, purple.*" Lulu hung up.

A Code Purple was surge capacity although it was unclear what that meant. Code White was Incident, so it was a little more specific. Sabine decided to go with White, for clarity's sake.

Telecomm, besides being buried in the windowless second sub-basement level, was not a part of the hospital that had ever been renovated. The walls were a shade of possibly foam green, with chipped shelves and an unframed bulletin board mounted over each of the three switchboard operators' desks. Task lighting came mostly from the small red lights on the fire control panel, the glow from the computer screens, a pale green from the police scanner and radio, and the icy blue from the code phone. A pulsing yellow from the gift shop panic panel warmed up the rest of the room. Sabine looked on Telecomm's decor as spaceship steampunk, like Battlestar Galactica, and she was fine with it.

Glo picked up the held call from the newspaper guy. "Fuck you too," she explained patiently, then quickly clicked onto the next call. "This is Operator Glo, how can I help you? Yes, Dr. Raj. Respiratory didn't answer her page? Okay, we'll find her. Yes, we'll find her stat." She clicked her headset to mute. "Sabine, did you page the RT?"

"Yes yes yes. I'll try paging her on the overhead, who knows, she might be in house."

"I'm flipping out here, Sabine, I think I just swore at someone. I want to do the Code White overhead."

"You did the last overhead, I'm doing the Code White."

The phone lines, five on each operator's computer, were pinging and blinking mercilessly.

"No, I didn't."

"You did, Glo, it was the Rapid Response page, remember?"

"Yes but now you got that call from Victor, so that's two."

"Okay, you page the RT and I'll page the code."

"Deal."

Glo clicked on the computer code opening an overhead page, slowed her breathing, lowered her voice, and pushed her retired flight attendant smile through the console microphone. "Your attention please. Respiratory to the ER, stat. Respiratory to the ER, stat."

Sabine noticed that Glo had the same expression on her face as the time four years ago, famous throughout Telecomm, when she had the affair with the fireman.

Sabine took a sip of cold coffee and made her voice lower and more airport-y than Glo's had been. "Attention all personnel, Code White. Attention all personnel, Code White."

Glo and Sabine looked at each other, actually breathed, and then did a high five.

A call from the ER lit up on the phone system. Sabine and Glo each rushed to answer it first. Sabine was faster. She had been there fifteen years, Glo twenty, and Sabine considered herself younger and more agile.

"This is the switchboard, Sabine speaking, how can I help you?" She was in her glory now, confident and in command. The switchboard at Telecomm had emerged into importance.

There was breathing on the other end.

Sabine lowered her voice another notch and slowed down her tempo. This was turning out to be a good day. "This is the hospital operator, is there someone there? Are you in distress?"

Then a whispery voice with the hint of an exotic accent. "*It's Juliet.*"

"Juliet! My God, girl, are you alright?"

"*There are sick and wounded people all around me.*"

"Yes, that happens in the ER."

"*A young girl, blood all over. I think I'm having a flashback.*"

"Is she by chance a gunshot victim do you know? Can you see her?"

"*Oh she's been shot alright.*" Juliet spoke in a soft monotone. "*I offered to help out, but they ignore me. The respiratory therapist is working on her and they're getting her ready for surgery.*"

Sabine covered her microphone and poked Glo. "The RT made it to the ER."

Glo nodded and turned back to her computer. "Operator Glo speaking, how can I help you?"

Sabine went back to her microphone. "Juliet, what did they say was wrong with you?"

"*They just got to dehydrated before the gunshot girl came in. I'm walking around though, I'm okay. I probably just missed Happy Hour or something.*"

"Listen, can you make it back to the condo? I have wine."

"I could call Mrs.T's Taxi, but I'm not dressed. Do you think that matters?"

"Oh better idea - take the elevator down to Telecomm, you can sit here while I finish out my shift and then I'll drive us home. Okay?"

"She's a young teenager, Sabine. From what I can tell, she was shot in the back and it went all the way through. The bullet came out her stomach. She was alert when they brought her in."

"Come to Telecomm. We'll debrief."

"I don't know how to get there."

"Just wander around, find elevators, and keep going down." Sabine pressed End Call and then picked up the next call in her queue. "Trummel Hospital, Sabine speaking, how can I help you?"

"Yes. I have PTSD and diabetes. I'm calling because I just chopped the end of my pinky off with a salad spinner."

"Can you get yourself to a hospital?"

"I guess."

"You'll have to get to Danverse-on-Hudson, the Trummel ER is closed off for right now. We're kind of on lockdown. Can you do that?"

In the background, over the police scanner that sat on a shelf between the workstations, a disembodied male voice announced in a monotone, *"Central to Trummel, person flipping out, eleven Oak Street. Charlie Level, lights no sirens. Person flipping out, eleven Oak Street. twenty-three twelve."*

Somewhere deep within the debris of a supply cabinet, a muted pager beeped. Sabine flashed on Swann's Way from Proust's *Remembrance of Things Past* - something about "The places we have known" being "only a thin slice among contiguous impressions which formed our life at that time…". And then, as she often did, she remembered dancing in Rio at Carnival in 1995.

Chapter 2

*Juliet was a trained nurse although her
certification had long ago expired.
Sabine had been shaped early on by Dr. Kildare,
and more recently by Dr. Who.*

Strange people inhabit the hospital at all times. That was the natural state of things in rural mid-state New York. Where else could anyone go, besides the Walmart? Non-linear was the new normal. If you couldn't adjust, then you belonged back in the City where it was safe

Still, Sabine thought, a shooting in the hospital parking lot? And now Victor calls and tells her to announce a Code Silver because the guy is running through the hospital with a gun. Who ran with a gun in Trummel, for godsake? Of course just about everyone had a gun in Trummel, but most people hid their bad manners by doing their shooting in private. "Let this guy come into Telecomm. He needs to learn some manners."

Glo snorted in agreement. "I mean, didn't his mother ever teach him not to shoot people? I raised three kids, all of them teenagers before they became adults."

One thing you learn early on in hospital work is to be careful how you narrate the Universe. Someone or some thing is always listening in. Everyone knows that if the phones are quiet and the police scanner has lulled, you're not supposed to act like anything is unusual. You have to display to the powers-that-be that you're totally comfortable with no emergencies, that everyone who didn't fall off the chairlift at the ski slope was supposed to remain unmaimed for that day and that the domestic rowdydow on Birch Street was actually someone watching *Night of the Living Dead* with the volume too loud.

If you say anything, like *Wow, it's really quiet today*, then all hell breaks loose.

Sabine didn't know exactly what universal law was being broken by making an innocent observation about a gun incident, but disturb the equilibrium she did. She had read enough Deepak Chopra to know that dark matter was made up of something that kept score.

So by even thinking that this guy with his gun should leave the patients alone, hide from Security and the Trummel police, and even more amazingly, locate Telecomm so his behavior could be adjusted by the switchboard operators, Sabine pretty much messed up. Of course she took it back immediately, looking up at the unlit fluorescent lightbulbs to where a Universal

Coordinating Department might be, and saying "I was only kidding, you know that, right?"

"You're able to contact outer space through the ceiling now?" Operator Glo looked at Sabine, then brushed back her long gray-brown hair and returned her gaze to her computer screen. "Thank you for calling Trummel Hospital, this is Operator Glo, how may I direct your call?" she said into her headset microphone. "You're having shrink-wrap rage? Hold on dear, I'll transfer you to the ER."

Sabine peeled her headset off and looked back up at the ceiling. It was a series of gray metal grids holding up pockmarked fiber tiles with stuff stuck in them: unused plant hanger hooks, mangled twist ties, assorted ducts, discolored spots from leaks, and a sprinkler. "Surely you can see past people's comments into their hearts and you know about my gratitude for Mother Theresa, my cats, and the Grateful Dead."

Juliet, who was sitting cross-legged on the engineer's desk in a dark corner in the back of the room, actually laughed. She had found her way down to Telecomm from the emergency room and made herself at home.

Sabine and Glo both looked back, having forgotten Juliet was there. Over Juliet's floor-length cream satin lingerie was a gray-green ER blanket, with her bare feet and red toenails sticking out.

Sabine explained, "I was just thinking the earth could be hit by a meteor at any time with no warning. A girl wants to keep current with her karma."

"Oh, that." Glo said, done with it. She turned her attention back to her computer and punched in the next caller. "Operator Glo speaking, how can I help you?"

"How do you know we aren't dead already?" Juliet was smoothing her fingers around a white Keep Calm and Thank an Engineer mug she found on the desk. "Maybe a meteor did hit, and we're all walking around not knowing we left the planet eons ago."

"In that case, wouldn't there be a sign or something?" Sabine said. "Like Commander Riker on the Starship Enterprise when he was stuck in an alternate reality and he was reminded that it was an illusion every time he saw a full moon?"

Juliet looked down for a beat, as if a switch of recognition had been activated. Then she caught Sabine's eye and smiled warmly at her for the first time. "Yes. Like that."

Sabine stood up. Her work here was done. She had impressed her beautiful neighbor, the goddess Juliet Indigo. "All right, then. I'm making coffee. Ladies, coffee?"

"Ya think?" Glo said. "No, not you, Sir, sorry. Room 340? Right away. Yeah, sorry, sorry."

"I don't want to be any trouble," Juliet said. "I'll make the coffee, Sabine, you go back to your switchboard." She slid out of her blanket and off the metal desktop. "Any word on that poor girl who was shot?"

"We're operating in the dark." Sabine stretched her arms up in the air and inhaled deeply, to jostle the kinks out. "Just bits and pieces. We'll have the whole picture at some point. At least she's alive."

"We're groping," Glo clarified. "At least we haven't killed her yet."

"K-cups are in this cabinet." Sabine opened a cabinet behind Juliet. A baggie of plastic forks fell out onto the fax machine and a soft cloud of what was probably prehistoric sugar drifted out into the room. Juliet coughed. Sabine plugged herself back into her desk. "We've just run out of cream. Oh well."

Over the police scanner, the handsome disembodied male voice said, "*Seizure in the Looney Bin, delta level. Seizure in the Looney Bin, delta level, O-four-hundred.*"

Sabine loved her job. Every night she happily disappeared into the yellowing, ancient fuselage-like compartment that was buried deep in the interior of the hospital complex. She loved the coziness of the windowless switchboard office. She, Glo, and Aja, the third night shift operator, felt special because they had table lamps on the consoles which gave their desks an amber, cave-like glow. With the glittering lights from the police scanner, Telecomm was transformed into a post-apocalyptic torch-lit chamber. Sabine knew if her clothes were covered in cat hair, no one would be able to tell. Also they had a Keurig coffeemaker and all the hospital beeper batteries. Breathable air was scarce, but there was plenty of hand sanitizer. She hoped this was enough to keep Juliet impressed.

The three women jumped when a stranger's form filled the switchboard office doorway.

"Oh - I'm sorry." A pale, freckled young woman with big, frizzy red hair took a step back into the hall. She was wearing baggy jeans and a camisole, over which was a sheer orange tunic with one shoulder falling off. "I guess I'm lost." Her voice was unnaturally high, like a child.

Glo peeled her headset off and went to the door. "It's alright, hon, it's easy to get lost in this place." She went seamlessly into caretaker mode, which sufficed for excitement when emergency mode wasn't appropriate. She motioned for the young woman to come in, and dragged the empty third switchboard chair toward the door, as bait. "We're making coffee. Where were you trying to get to?"

The young woman didn't move from the door. She was breathing heavily and she had a black leather jacket over one arm. "Um, oh. I'm not sure."

Not to be outdone by Glo's sudden earth mother mode, Sabine turned her chair around to face the woman and said "What's your name, dear? We'll help you." Then one of Sabine's phone lines rang and she went back to her computer. "Thank you for calling Trummel Hospital, okay, hold on, we'll get someone to untangle you. You're welcome" as she punched in a beeper number and then switched off her call.

"So are you guys the operators?" the high small voice in the doorway asked.

"Yes. We are the operators," Glo assured her, as if she were saying *We're the healers in this place; you've found us at last.* "Come sit down and tell us what department you're looking for." She jiggled the top of the chair slightly as one might dangle a slice of turkey in front of a stray cat to get it to come in.

"I heard all kinds of things on the loudspeakers," the girl said. "Are you guys the security department?"

"We're the operators," Glo repeated patiently, now well into wise grandmother.

Juliet took a hot cup of steaming coffee from the Keurig and brought it to the young woman. "I used to be a nurse," Juliet whispered in meaningful subtext mode as she made direct eye contact with the girl.

Sabine finished up her call with "We don't have a specific medicine department per se, m'am, I mean this whole place is a hospital. No, there's no specific potassium department. Okay, you're welcome" and clicked off the call, then turned to face the door, her head tethered to the computer by the cord.

They had flirted with wireless headsets once when the budget director, Patty Horizon, was having a nervous breakdown and decided that doing update therapy on the hospital back rooms might make her feel more selfless. The wireless headsets quickly became part of the cupboard debris, though, because switchboard mythology had it that you got better connections when connected to things with wires. After all, they had corded telephones on *Battlestar Galactica*.

Sabine flashed on the thought that the three of them must look to this young woman like a pack of near-mad castaways who hadn't seen another human in decades.

"Come, sit, hon, don't be shy." Glo was still jiggling Aja's empty switchboard chair. "Anywhere you need to call, we can do that for you. Patients' rooms, nurses' stations, you name it. Oh my God."

"What?" Sabine said.

"We were supposed to do a Code Silver for the guy running around with the gun, remember?"

"Oh my God," Sabine said.

Immediately both women lunged for the microphone, which was sitting between their desks. Glo was sixty-two, a retired flight attendant who had recently had knee surgery. Sabine was sixty-four and had recently pulled something trying to do the dolphin plank pose in her livingroom to a YouTube video by yin yoga guru Hiba Almodóvar. They both hobbled madly to the mike.

The young redhead jumped out of the way with a soft, high-pitched spider alert-type yelp. Sabine grabbed the microphone. Glo recovered instantly, smiled maniacally, and stood in the doorway so their guest wouldn't run off. Juliet got her ER blanket from the engineer's desk and thought she might put it around someone.

"Attention all personnel." Sabine was at her most resonant. "Code Silver. Attention all personnel. Code Silver. Thank you. Thank you."

"What's a Code Silver?" The young girl scrunched close to the door, shoulders and arms tensed so as not to brush against Glo. Sabine thought she looked like a pale little lost waif with a frightened six-year old voice. Something was definitely going on with this creature.

"Oh now, it's nothing, really," Glo said and put an arm over the shirking girl's shoulder. "It's just a precaution."

"We're very careful," Sabine added.

Juliet offered the blanket but the girl didn't budge.

"Okay," she squeaked, "But what does it mean? I mean, I'm sorry if I'm disturbing your work."

"Are you alright?" Sabine asked. It occurred to her that since this girl was lost in the hospital she might actually have a medical situation that needed tending.

"Well, um, I was just wondering if the shooting victim was still alive. I'm sorry I don't mean to be nosy or anything."

Glo and Sabine stared at the girl. The switchboard phones were ringing and blinking.

"Yes, what *is* a Code Silver?" Juliet echoed.

"It's nothing," Glo snapped. She sat at her desk and attached herself back to the computer. "Thank you for calling Trummel Hospital, this is Operator Glo, how can I help you?"

The girl looked to Sabine.

Sabine sighed. "I mean, it might be a gun alert. Type thing." She was getting tired. Emergencies were great, but when they dragged on they lost their vigor.

"Just a second." She put her headset on and clicked quickly through a few calls. Sweating, she pulled the headset off again and silently cursed at the thought that her long, silky brown hair that she had spent forty-five minutes blow-drying that morning, now probably looking like *The Madwoman of Chaillot.* And her straight bangs were probably now parted in the middle with one side sticking up, like they did as her shift wore on. Headset hair. She swiveled her chair around.

The young girl was standing in the corner by the door jamb, sobbing softly.

Sabine stood up and tried to take one of the girl's hands, but she held them tight over her eyes. "Don't be scared, sweetie," Sabine mustered, "we have crazy people running around the hospital all the time, it's not a problem. They'll find the gunman, I promise you. We have our own security force, his name is Victor, and the Trummel police are here. They're very handsome."

The girl pulled away from Sabine and as she did, something fell out of the leather jacket she had over her arm. It landed with a heavy thud on the tattered remains of what used to have been perhaps a carpet. It was large and not immediately identifiable. Glo, Juliet, and Sabine stared at it. The girl stopped sobbing. Telecomm was suddenly silent except for the mad ringing of the ten phone lines and *"...have a report of a severed thumb in the grinder at The Black Cat. Copy that..."* coming in over the police scanner.

It was a gun.

"I'm not comprehending this," Sabine said, looking from the waif to the gun.

Juliet was all over it. She swooped down, picked up the gun, and slid back to her engineer's desk where she jammed it into the top drawer and then stood guard in front of it. Sabine figured Juliet's quick reflexes were from her Vietnam PTSD.

"Your mother must be so proud," Glo mumbled in a jaded monotone.

"Oh God, I'm so sorry," the girl whispered. Frizzy wisps of red hair stuck to her face from the sobbing.

She could bring out the blue in her eyes with some gel eyeliner, Sabine thought for a brief moment as she reached for the radio pager, and a few dabs of hair serum. Put the hair in a pony tail, and go with a matte pink lip. "Switchboard to security. Code Silver in Telecomm. Switchboard to security, Code Silver in Telecomm, hello? Can we hurry?"

"I'm sure it was an accident," Juliet called from the back of the room.

"Security to switchboard." It was Victor. A blessed male hero voice. Rich and reassuring, wearing an official badge, coming to make everything all better.

"Acknowledged." Kill me now, thought Sabine, I'm so freaking lonely.

It was Sabine and her three cats and her nice couch and premium cable and of course the Merlot. The nightmares had started early on, but had intensified after her third marriage. Just last night, an enormous hairy rainforest spider was waiting in the shower to abduct her cats. She couldn't call the handsome, capable 911 guys because she didn't have her makeup on. The spider, being from the equatorial jungle, would leap through the air toward you, so you'd have to run out of the bathroom, slam the door shut, jam laundry under the door, and simply never use that room again ever in the history of the planet. But then you couldn't find your cats, so you'd have to go back into the bathroom to make sure the cats weren't in there. This was why it was important to live in a two-bathroom condo.

"I just want to tell you one thing," said the waif, her speech uneven from swallowing too much air.

"Can guns go off by themselves?" Sabine whispered.

"No. It's in the drawer." Juliet had now come into her own. Her voice was firm and knowledgeable, her stance in front of the engineer's desk was military. She nearly glowed in her creamy satin nightgown, like an archangel descended to earth to straighten out all her adorable pet savages.

Sabine could almost see the wind blowing Juliet's hair back in slow motion, if it weren't still in an updo.

"It won't go off by itself," Juliet said. "Well, it could have gone off when it was dropped, but it didn't."

"I'm sorry to be a bother," said the young woman, pulling herself together. "I just need to explain this to you."

Glo gave a snort of contempt, a sort of sharp half-laugh. "After all we've done for you."

"No need to make her mad," Sabine said to Glo in exaggerated nonchalance. Then to the girl, "Tell us what, dear?"

The girl looked from Sabine to Glo to Juliet as if seeing them for the first time. "You're making fun of me."

"Did you shoot that teenager?" Juliet called sternly from her position in the back of Telecomm.

Then, as if she just had a revelation, the girl said, "You must think I'm horrible!"

"We're Switchboard," Sabine assured her.

But Sabine wasn't actually too sure. Her training was holding, though. Not just her hospital training, which kept her demeanor smooth, despite the rainforest spiders, but also her spiritual training which was a cocktail made from a Transcendental Meditation course she took in the early seventies; studying near-death experiences with Elizabeth Kubler Ross the death guru with her macrobiotic friend in Cambridge, Mass in the eighties; and the book *Autobiography of a Yogi* which was required reading for all baby boomers back in the day.

Then thankfully, Victor's large uniformed frame filled the doorway. Behind him was Eusebio, the other security guard on duty that night, and a Trummel police officer. No one moved as Victor swept his trained gaze over the room. "Who's this?" he said, nodding toward the waif.

"I'm Clea." Her voice sounded like she was imitating a mouse for the amusement of a baby.

"So?" Victor said.

"I know," Clea answered. "Exactly, right?" Clea darted to Victor, as if running for safety from the Mean Girls, and Victor reflexively put his arm around her.

"This is our Code Silver," Sabine explained.

Clea looked up at Victor. "Is the shooting victim alive?" she asked. "Is she okay?"

Victor hugged her to him. Evidently "This is our Code Silver" hadn't computed.

"You're Clea?" Victor said to his new little charge. "Are you okay? Did you see the gunman?"

Then to Sabine, who was frozen in a state of Zen groundlessness, "Where's the shooter?"

"It was an accident," Clea said.

Victor looked down. "Are you a witness? Were you hurt?"

"I kind of shot her," Clea said. "I feel terrible. Is Denize still alive?"

Information. Incoming: The shooting victim's name was Denize; Juliet had quick reflexes; Victor was an idiot; the cop who was standing behind Eusebio was a young hunk; Sabine was glad she had recently re-touched the roots of her silky long chestnut hair, and had on an actual skirt and high heeled boots.

Chapter 3

Both Juliet and Sabine grew up watching foreign films. Juliet had been shaped early on by Godard's Pierrot le fou; *Sabine by Almodóvar's* Women on the Verge.

Juliet and Sabine were neighbors in what the Trummel zoning board lady called a condo, meaning there was no other place in town to live unless you wanted to roam aimlessly around a huge, dilapidated eighteenth century Victorian, get depressed, drink wine, and write poetry in the garden in the middle of the night looking for your cat. Sabine knew she couldn't live like that. The condo at least gave her the illusion of an ordered life, with recessed lighting in the kitchen and a phone number you could call if something broke. And her cats stayed inside because Sabine hated poetry. She had actually tried to write poetry at one point, but *The New Yorker* rejected it and she never looked back.

"So have you felt a major life change since tumbling through the portal last night?" Sabine pulled the sleeves of her pink hoodie over her hands to ward off the late afternoon November chill. She reached to the balcony coffee table and picked up her wine glass by the stem, through the hoodie fabric.

"Portal? Oh, the emergency room. No, not yet," Juliet said. "You?"

"Me? No, I'm a rock," said Sabine. "How are you feeling?"

"Like smoking. But that part of my life is done with. I'm evolving. I guess I'll have to settle for the wine." Juliet took a sip from her wine glass. An orange maple leaf blew gently across the wooden slats of the patio floor.

"So what did they say was wrong with you?" Sabine said.

"Oh it's silly. I actually prefer ayurvedic medicine."

"You don't want to talk about it."

"No."

"That's fine. I mean if there's anything I can do, I have connections."

Juliet paused for a moment as if making a decision to confide in her new friend. "My dream consciousness was trying to impinge on waking consciousness," Juliet said. "I became dehydrated. Out here in Trummel, New York, with no acupuncturist."

Sabine flashed on how best to proceed. She needed to extract information that was more user-friendly. The whole consciousness thing was too huge. She went with: "You used to be a nurse. With the army, in Vietnam?"

"Yes."

Sabine waited for further intel, but it wasn't coming. Still, having wine on Juliet's balcony on the fourth floor of their five-story high-rise, overlooking the parking lot, was nice. It was autumn, rich with the smell of wood burning fireplaces from surrounding family homes. "So what was the actual diagnosis?" she prompted. "Like, can you pass out from consciousness issues?"

"Oh you know."

"Well anyway. You're feeling better, that's the important thing."

"I had a lover in Paris twenty-five years ago. He wore a black leather jacket and rode a motorcycle. We were strangers, it was heady. I'm glad I had the experience, especially now that it's long gone."

"Yes," Sabine sighed. This was going to be a high maintenance friendship, meaning she realized she would have a hard time keeping up. "I remember Frank Zappa's *Don't Eat the Yellow Snow* like it was yesterday."

"I could never take a lover in Trummel," Juliet replied. It wasn't a complaint, but rather a soft, dreamy fact. Serene, without emotion, just noting the situation. "I still have a husband, you know."

"Oh, yes, of course." Sabine was desperate to know what was going on with that, but didn't want to jinx the new friendship by prying. She forced herself to be still for a second. Then she said "I'm thinking of joining a dating service."

"Yes. Go for it, Sabine."

"I've had husbands of course. But now I miss the drama."

"You're a dispatcher and call center operator at the hospital. You're in the center of all the drama."

"You're right, Juliet. It's just that I need signs of life around me. Everyone at the hospital is sick."

"Ah yes."

"So did they give you medication or anything?"

"After Paris?"

"No, from the ER. You said they said you were dehydrated?"

"Probably." Juliet stood up. "I'm going in to get some slippers. Shall I bring out some food of some sort?"

"Do you have any?"

"No, do you?"

"No, I eat at the hospital."

Juliet tugged open the sliding glass door and stepped inside. Soft electronic beats from her Brazilification Chillout Lounge Pandora station escaped onto the balcony, then muted as she closed the door behind her.

Sabine took her wine and walked to the balcony railing. She leaned over.

"Hey! Trauma Town Dispatcher!" a young male voice called up to the balcony from the parking lot. It was Lile, the condo's handyman and pizza delivery coordinator. A cigarette was hanging from his left hand. "How's it going?"

"Good, Lile. You?" Sabine called down. Her hoodie had *Trauma Town Dispatch* printed on the front, Trauma instead of Trummel. Their voices echoed in the chill.

"How come you're not at the hospital?"

"We kind of had an incident yesterday. I'm in recovery."

"Okay then. You go, Trauma Town!" He laughed and disappeared into his mud-streaked pickup.

Within the mansion-esque enclosure of centuries-old maples, oaks, and elms surrounding the condo like acoustical tiles, Lile's truck starting was crisp and present. He backed up, then drove off.

Across the street in the park, Sabine heard muted laughter and yelling from children running around in their fall coats, playing, swinging, sliding, going about their business. She let her thoughts go and just inhaled deeply. Streetlights were starting to go on. She had a weird darkness in the pit of her stomach.

Juliet floated back onto the balcony, still in her bare feet. Over her blue oriental robe she had added a long string of pearls and a hit of Chanel Cristalle. She had a new bottle of wine, and topped off both glasses from it, even though there was the half-empty bottle on the glass coffee table. Sabine's darkness went away.

Juliet dropped into her chair and sipped her wine, leaving dusky matte pink lipstick on her glass. "So Sabine, I heard that the gunshot surgery was successful. The child is going to be okay?" she asked in a soft Uma Thurman *Henry and June* art film voice. "How is she doing?"

"She's in the ICU. Yeah, they saved her so far." Sabine matched Juliet's low whisper. "Here's the thing. There was a dimensional shift in the hospital when they were first working on her in the ER. Did you notice that?"

"Yes." Juliet took a thoughtful sip and gazed into the distance. "What do you mean?"

"Everyone changed. It was a complete one eighty. We were all going about our catastrophes and shredding and normal daily stuff, and then when they brought Denize in with her gunshot wound - she was so close to death. It was like every person in the hospital dropped all their stuff and focused completely on keeping her alive. Like an ultimate tunnel vision. Like nothing mattered in anyone's universe except this girl's life."

"I felt it too, Sabine, I think."

"You did. You got up from your ER bed and went to help. It was like a different dimension dropped onto the hospital, like the Borg where everyone shares the same consciousness."

Juliet perked up. "Ah yes, the Borg."

"Our job was to save this girl's life. And answer phones. That's it. All thoughts of doctors' bad handwriting on prescriptions and why their prescriptions are not computerized like the rest of the world, all issues with social workers never answering their pagers, frustrations over the lab's new automated telephone answering tree - all that stuff went untouched. We were unified. And I was part of it."

"I'm having palpitations."

"What?"

"It's nothing."

"Maybe we should eat something."

"Let's just drink."

"Okay."

"I'm just a little tense," Sabine explained to Aja the next day as the two were manning second shift. "Trying to stay calm is extremely stressful."

"Tell me about it," Aja sympathized. Her right hand, as usual, was gripping her mouse and clicking maniacally on anything that moved. She had once explained it as MMS, mosquito mouse syndrome, but Aja was so agreeable and sweet that no one ever bothered about her quirks. She was a vegan and her parents had named her after the Steely Dan song.

Telecomm was dark as usual, even though it was two in the afternoon. The switchboard room was one of those subterranean places where you descend into a zone and put on your headset for eight hours, like a coal miner. There was not much call to leave the second level basement, everything they needed was right there: a small fridge, a microwave for popcorn, of course the Keurig, a fire extinguisher, and a toaster oven. Above the toaster oven, written in black marker, was taped a note: "NOTHING IS TO BE PUT ON TOP OF THE TOASTER OVEN," which was, of course, the "Don't Shoot This Sign" of Telecomm. Atop the toaster oven was the remnant of a plant, and a row of little plastic ducks wearing stethoscopes.

Handwritten post-its and signs printed in Comic Sans font on the backs of emergency call sheets were tacked around the room as needed. A Prozac notepad was velcroed next to the code phone for when hospital workers called in with their patients' heart attacks and seizures. A special form was also there in case a social worker called in with a Code Amber, which was the missing patient code. You had to prompt the social worker for the information: child or adult, where did they go missing, what were they wearing. And a dry erase board had been hung next to the fire panel so when a Code Red came in you could write down what was on fire. They had meant to re-name all the hospital stairwells because two weeks earlier Sabine announced a Code Red in Stairwell 6, but no one knew where Stairwell 6 was and Facilities had to find a blueprint but by that time the Fire Department just went where the smoke was. And then Denize LeClair came in with her gunshot wound and everyone forgot about renaming the stairwells.

"You know that woman who shot the teenager – she was here in Telecomm," Sabine said. "The shooter."

"I know I heard," Aja said. "Oops, excuse me." She turned to her computer and spoke as if to an intimate lover. "Thank you for calling Trummel Hospital, this is Aja, how may I assist you today?"

Sabine took a sip of her coffee and turned to her own computer. "Thank you for calling – you what? You

want to eat your head? Hold please." She clicked the
hold button and took another sip of coffee, did a yoga
neck roll, then clicked back onto the call. "Oh, okay,
you were kidding, so how can I help you? You're
having a heart attack? Hold please." Sabine's hands
moved fast and effortlessly, like Data from Star Trek
Next Generation assembling a spaceship panel to keep
the Enterprise from blowing up. She transferred the
caller to the emergency room, which was a safer
strategy than having him hang up and call 911. Having
him hang up risked losing him and it was better that
Lulu lost him.

"Your son is in jail?," Aja was saying to her new
caller. "This is the hospital, m'am, you'd have to call the
jail, right? Yep. You're welcome."

A lull. Aja turned to Sabine and did a theatrical
sigh of mock mutual understanding, then waited to see
if Sabine would be forthcoming with more information
about the shooter.

"My neighbor Juliet grabbed the gun after it fell
to the floor," Sabine complied. "She's a Vietnam vet."

"Wow," Aja prodded.

"Yeah, I know. And then Victor and Eusebio
were here with the police. In a million years I wouldn't
have thought this woman could have shot anyone. I
could picture her, say, running a puppy daycare
center."

Aja shook her head. "You know, Sabine, it's perfectly normal to be stressed out after something like that." Aja was twenty-five.

"I offered the shooter coffee," Sabine answered.

"I heard. But look at least Denize is alive, and the shooter is – somewhere safe, right?"

Sabine felt an annoyance tugging at her. Aja was trying to put everything in place, and Sabine wasn't going to fall for it. Aja was two generations younger than anyone in Telecomm. She was lacking a necessary angst; a permanently imbedded horror. Maybe she never saw *Bambi*.

The switchboard lit up. Aja disappeared into a call.

"Trummel Hospital." Sabine took her own call in the flight attendant voice she sometimes copied from Operator Glo. "How can I help you?"

"It's Raphael from The Sun again. Sabine, right? How is your teenage patient doing today?"

"You know I'm not allowed to tell anyone anything. Why are you not calling Barbara Vermouth from PR? We already went through this. Barbara handles the public."

"I know, I know, I know. I'm sorry. Barbara doesn't answer her phone and I just need something to

put in the paper. Anything. I'm hanging on by a thread here, Sabine."

"Are you crying?"

"I could. I'm from the East Village. I'm dying a slow death here in the outer territories."

"Oh awesome. I'm from Brooklyn."

Sabine heard a sigh on Raphael's end.

"I didn't mean awesome that you're dying a slow death," she said. "I'm sorry."

"It's alright."

"So do you want to leave another message on Barbara's voicemail?"

"Yes, Sabine, that is what I want to do."

And then Sabine and Aja both sat up straight. The scent of Avon *Exotic Nights* was seeping into Telecomm, attached to a brisk clicking of high heels on what used to be carpet but was now closer to bare concrete. "Gotta go," Sabine said to Raphael, and clicked EndCall. "Aja! Incoming!"

"Already noted," said Aja.

And then Nyx, the Sub-Basement Level Information Officer, stood in the doorway.

"Oh my God, Nyx," Sabine burst out. "How is Denize Leclair?"

But Nyx tensed up and Sabine realized that in her hunger for information she had broken protocol. Information officers were into protocol. They knew they were essential to the smooth running of the hospital; they knew they were the most important people in the facility – except for the doctors and nurses, and alright the lab geeks and respiratory techs – and they demanded acknowledgment of that. You don't give them the respect, you don't get the Intel you need. It was part of office politics.

Aja cleared the air. "God, you look gorgeous today, Nyx. I love your earrings." Aja's left eye clicked shut tight and when it opened her head twitched as if she were shaking a mosquito off her cheek. Everyone knew it was from her cold turkey stopping of the Prolexa she had been on since her teen years. She dismissed it laughingly as her self-diagnosed EBSS - electro-brain snapping syndrome. She had described it to Sabine and the other operators as tiny electric shocks in her brain. Pretty much all the time. When she first quit the Prolexa it was huge – she felt zapping sensations in her brain a few times a minute. "Zzzp," she described it. "Zzzp." Now, a few years later, it was not as pronounced, but it was there. Like mini-seizures all the time. She said it was fine, just something that was part of her day-to-day reality, like watching *Grey's Anatomy* or brushing her teeth. "Those earrings sparkle like real diamonds," she said to Nyx.

Nyx visibly relaxed, totally ignoring Aja's tic.
"Thanks, Aja. They're two carats each. Genuine cubic
zirconium."

"Ah, beautiful," said Sabine.

Nyx smiled and disassembled the shredder.
"Okay, here's what's up with our little Denize."

As Nyx dumped the shredded patient
information into the large white trash bag she carried, a
lock of her golden hair came loose from her French
twist and fell into her face. She was pretty, and Sabine
always admired the ease she had when she was
around men.

Sabine herself was nervous around the security
guards because they were good looking, or at least
they had that aura about them there in the hospital, in
their element. You find a few missing toddlers for ER
patients, you handcuff a few drunken spouses visiting
the ICU, you build up a certain confidence that
translates into good looks. When you're on your own
turf, you can strut. You may look completely forgettable
at the Walmart, but there in Trauma Town, you were
who everyone turned to for help.

Nyx laughed with all the handsome guys,
whispered funny stuff to them that made them smile,
always exchanged what looked like intimate info with
them, although when Sabine overheard those

conversations she realized it was nothing more than what the soup of the day was in the cafeteria.

Aja said, "Okay, Nyx, we don't have much time."

Nyx put the shredder back together and picked up the trash. "She's very weak, but so far they say she's going to be okay. You should have seen all the blood in the OR, it was gushing. Dr. Raj was yelling at everyone and the whole place – oh she's on North 3 by the way, Room 322. She's not able to really eat yet, because you know, she has a complete hole in her middle, but –"

"And what's up with the shooter?" Sabine asked. "Is she at all sane? Clea?"

"Oh my God," Nyx said. This was going to be good, because Nyx sat down in Operator Glo's chair and peeled off her non-latex gloves so she could fix her hair. Sabine and Aja leaned in to make a sacred information circle. Nyx's voice went down an octave and she smiled slightly, narrowing her eyes, in the know. "She's in custody."

"And what's poor Denize's story?" Sabine whispered into the circle, still desperate for details, and knowing time was slipping by. Nyx would have to be leaving Telecomm soon to clean the bathrooms in the ER.

Nyx looked at Sabine and then Aja and smiled from deep within, as if she were a queen giving out federal grants to her subjects. Sabine noticed that Nyx had a golden aura about her, a pulsing, sparkling glow. It was because Nyx was an information gateway. When you know things, you have power, and then you have a golden aura, and then you have control over your life. And then you don't have to worry about your cats when you're at work. Perhaps at that point you have people. Something happens, it's okay.

Nyx said, "Denize - she does have people. They're *from* somewhere." Then she got up, put her non-latex gloves back on, and said, "I'll keep you posted" as she disappeared into the mists of the hallway.

Over the scanner a male voice said, *"Car fell into the lake, delta level. Car in the lake, delta level. Nineteen twenty-nine."*

Sabine imagined the man attached to this self-assured disembodied voice to be thirty-five-ish, wearing a uniform of some sort, taking his hero role seriously but not self-consciously. When he pushed the talk button on his radio, his upper arm muscles would flex slightly, creating a wake of ripples through his broad chest. Clean-shaven. A non-smoker.

Chapter 4

Sabine's life had been shaped early on by Edward Albee's The Zoo Story.

At one minute to four the next morning, Sabine stretched and knocked Freddie Mercury off the bed. The alarm was set for four, and Sabine turned it off before it rang so as not to have to endure its nerve-splitting jolt. She had set the alarm sound to harp glissando, but it was still piercing. Freddie meowed and ran to the food dish.

Sabine kept her three cats' food, water, and litter box in her bedroom in case of the apocalypse. Should, say, the Milky Way's black hole suddenly expand, she could stash the cats in the bedroom and shut the door, and they would be safe and have all their stuff. This system was designed for any sort of calamity, and gave Sabine the false sense of security she needed to keep from worrying about them when she was at the hospital.

"Aww, Freddie," she purred, and put her bare feet on the soft carpet. "Let's make some nice coffee."

Four a.m. was okay because Sabine was a night owl, and four was still the middle of the night. On days that she had to get up at eight for the second shift, for instance, that was difficult – but this week her shift began at 5:30 a.m. She wouldn't see daylight until she got out at three, but it was November so it didn't matter. It would be gray and chilly. The leaves had turned and were now at the dull end of spectacular. It was the same every year - insidious in its predictability.

Sabine was always on the edge of an unidentifiable, unspecified panic. It filled her at night in her dreams, manifesting as invading insects frothing at the mouth, or the planet's wine stash going missing, or the discovery that Freya, her cat when she was eight, was still alive all this time and hadn't been fed.

The dreams shadowed her when she woke at four a.m., but she shook them off with coffee and cats. She had read enough Pirsig's *Zen and the Art of Motorcycle Maintenance* to know that there was more stuff going on than her mere nightmares, and with enough intel she could figure it out.

She'd have to check with Juliet about this, though, to be sure. Juliet had a handle on systems.

Sabine made a mental note to ask Juliet about the *Shore Leave Planet* from *Star Trek Next Gen* where the crew has R and R, but it turns out all their experiences are generated by a few computer guys in an underground lab.

"I'm okay without a life partner," Sabine had confided in Juliet the evening before during their happy hour on Juliet's balcony overlooking the parking lot.

"They come and go, right?" Juliet smiled and looked off into the distance, as if she were secretly looking out over Montmartre from atop the Cathedral de Sacré Coeur. "Anyway, I don't care. I'm deep into denial and it's been a godsend."

Sabine felt she had a lot to learn from Juliet. Juliet had had a lover in Paris and had helped re-attach limbs in Vietnam. Sabine had had a husband in Brooklyn who had had a lover in the Bronx. It was uncanny.

Then of course there was the discovery that Juliet liked the exact same red wine – Fire Station Red Engine Company 5 – and, like Sabine, always kept a week's worth stashed in the kitchen cabinet just in case a hurricane hit or she was very thirsty. Things were falling into place.

Freddie Mercury's meows segued into hungry howls. He was a huge orange tabby, and understood well how to manipulate the mother figure. Sabine emerged from her warm bedroom. She made a mental note not to step in cat vomit in her bare feet, but alas that was not to be. Dr. Crusher, the tiny gray tabby, had a delicate system.

Sabine fed Freddie and Dr. Crusher, and pulled on a pair of black silk slacks and a soft beige knit top while hopping around the condo looking for Higgs-Boson, the biter and the final member of the swarm. Then she headed out into the dark morning to run the Trummel Hospital communication engine.

In the moonless five a.m. gray northeast, Sabine parked in the ER lot, stepped out of her VW bug onto a sheet of black ice and smashed her arm, grabbing the open car door to keep from falling. Then she doubled up her scarf and crunched up her shoulders against the early chill, and began the careful shuffle to the emergency room entrance. Dim lighting reflected hazy sparkles on the bare, damp tree branches and bounced off ice crystals on the windows of the third shift nurses' cars.

On the other side of the parking lot was the gray silhouette of a young girl walking a small puppy. The girl leaned down to pat the small dog. "Do you love mama?" she said, a *sotto voce* off in the distance. Sabine walked past the large, lonely Emergency Room sign on the old brick of the building, and paused to give the automatic door a moment to figure out that it was supposed to open.

Inside the warm safety of the brightly lit ER, Sabine made her way through the hobbling, the groaning bandaged, the retching, the hemorrhaging, and the foaming at the mouth - she had studied Transcendental Meditation in Boston in the seventies – and drifted into the main part of the building which smelled of hot coffee, floor cleaner, and popcorn.

The idea of the hospital coffee as a warmfuzzy was an illusion, of course. You'd have to be in the midst of a narcoleptic crisis to drink it. "Thank You for the Keurig," Sabine said aloud to the hallway ceiling and headed for the elevator down to Telecomm.

As she entered Telecomm, the fire panel was false alarming again. "Good morning, Aja," Sabine said over the high-pitched beeping.

Aja was talking loudly into her headset. "It's Saturday, sir. 5:30. Yes, it's morning. You're welcome." She turned to Sabine. "Back at ya. Oops, looks like someone burnt the toast."

The beeping turned seamlessly into a full whoop, and the fire panel lit up with flashing red lights. Out in the hall, Sabine heard the fire doors slam shut and saw the white strobe lights burst into action. Yanina, the Utilization Review nurse in the office down the hall from Telecomm, came running in shrieking, "Is this a drill? I have to meet a social worker about a suicide!"

Sabine slid into her chair, put on her headset, and quickly logged onto her computer.

Aja followed protocol, picked up the microphone, and clicked into the hospital-wide paging system. "Attention all personnel." Her voice was young, high-pitched, and monotone. "Code Red in the ..." She whipped off one of her headset ears. "Sabine, where is the fire?"

Sabine spun around to check the fire panel on the wall behind her. "It says Wing 2, Level 4."

Yanina had commandeered the Keurig in the back of the switchboard room by the engineer's desk. "It couldn't be Level four," she said, "They probably mean Level three."

"Wing 2, Level 4," Aja continued her announcement.

The two-way radio came alive. *"Facility to Switchboard."*

Sabine reached for the radio microphone. "This is the Switchboard, go ahead Facility."

"It's Tom from Facilities. There is no Wing 2 on the fourth level."

The handsome male police scanner voice was detailing an overdose on Main Street and then continued with chest pains at the Walmart. The background sound of tinny sirens accompanied him each time his voice came on.

"I told you," said Yanina.

"Okay, copy," said Sabine to Tom. "Can you come to Telecomm? The panel says Wing 2 Level 4, so I don't know where the fire is."

"Could be level one," said Yanina. "These things are tricky."

"Be right there," said Tom.

"Thank you for calling Trummel Hospital." Sabine picked up the next incoming call. "How can I help you?"

"My phone won't hang up."

"I'm sorry?"

"I got some sort of automated call from you guys, and I hung up, and now every time I pick up the phone, there you are. It won't hang up."

"Okay, thank you for telling us."

With the fire panel still whooping, Sabine made her way to the Keurig and powered it up. "Coffee, Aja?"

"Just hot water, thanks. My mom tucked some Indian Rose Petal teabags into my backpack this morning."

Sabine went to the switchboard room's door and looked down the hall. Tom from Facilities was coming, followed by a maintenance guy and a guy from Plant. They wore jeans with T-shirts and stomachs billowing over tool belts. "False alarm," Tom called. They were walking in a line. Sabine thought of the Grateful Dead and the Doo Dah Man.

"Okay." Sabine turned toward Aja. "You can dismiss the Code, it was a false alarm."

"Attention all personnel," Aja's voice echoed over the loudspeakers. "Code Red dismissed. Attention all personnel. Code Red dismissed."

Yanina waited by the Keurig while a thin band of streaming coffee dripped into her *You'd Drink Too If You Were a Utilization Review Nurse* mug. "Ah. False alarm. I knew it." She pulled the hot mug from the machine, took a bold sip, and quickly fanned her mouth with her free hand. "Oh, Sabine. Now I remember why I was here. I was just in the ER and Lulu said to tell you she needs a new battery for her pager."

"Right now?"

"Yes? Hello?"

Sabine reached for the battered cardboard box on the floor under her desk and began rummaging through it, looking for a battery. "Aja, are you okay here by yourself while I run up to the ER?" She unearthed a sparkling blue Cyracom language translation phone that had never been used and was now out of date, a tangle of unruly black cables, a dusty plastic duck dressed like an EMT, and a double A battery.

"Yes I'm cool," Aja said to Sabine. She turned back to her computer. "Thank you for calling Trummel

Hospital, how can I help you? You want to speak to Heather? I need a last name, we have seventeen Heathers ... Do you have a last name? No? Well, is she a patient or an employee?... Oh. That means is she sick or does she work here...You're not sure?"

Clutching her battery, Sabine, still coffee-less, tore herself away from the warmth of the Battlestar bridge and stepped into the alternate universe of the fluorescent-lit hall. Trummel Hospital and Battlestar Galactica were the only two places she knew where the command to leap into another dimension was given through a corded landline.

Lulu was by the ambulance door, helping two handsome paramedics get a heart attack off the stretcher and onto a hospital gurney. Lulu and the handsome guys were exchanging important information as they wheeled the patient into an exam room, but Lulu was married, plus she saw guys like this all day, so the significance of her being able to talk to them so effortlessly was lost on her. "Wait for me, Sabine," Lulu said as the three of them disappeared with their cardiac arrest into Exam Room 3.

Sabine sat on a scratched faded yellow plastic chair by the door. A few seconds later Dr. Raj sped by and into the exam room, and then the paramedics came out. And there she was, there with two handsome guys – as opposed to being in Telecomm with her disembodied handsome police scanner voice. Sabine stood up for no reason and then felt faint as an arrhythmia kicked in.

"Hey. How's it going," one of the paramedics said to Sabine.

Now why, she wondered, at the age of 64, with three marriages behind her and any number of affairs – why was this guy thing so difficult? It didn't used to be. But Sabine had been in Trummel for 15 years, and with each passing year of no man in her life she became exponentially more desperate. Not lonely, mind you. She was fine without a man. But there was a certain mortal desperateness that had kicked in over the years that turned every hello from a male paramedic into her own massive psychoHormone spill.

"I'm good," Sabine said casually. "You?"

Okay, so that was over. Sabine fixed Lulu's beeper and then she was in the hall pushing for the elevator to get back down to Telecomm. When the elevator pinged and the door opened, that's when she saw Denize Leclair.

At first glance she didn't know who it was. But patients don't usually wander around the building in their hospital gowns, especially teenagers with massive bandaging around their middles out of which oozed thick globs of blood. Sometimes patients escaped, but the floor nurses kept a pretty good eye on things, so the escapees never got far. Still, the Code Amber, which was the missing patient code, was something hospital personnel took quite seriously, ever since Mr. Svod who was in for an insulin overdose, got out the front door and all the way to Main Street in his wheelchair, wearing his hospital gown and of course missing the one leg, before he was found. Risk Management had put out a flurry of red-flagged emails after that, and everyone was told to memorize which codes went with which disaster.

But there, right in front of her, was Denize, the teenager who was now locally famous for having been shot. Sabine knew it was Denize because their eyes locked and something transpired. The girl was clutching the elevator railing, bent over, half falling down. She had straight, dark hair, thick and cut short and blunt. Her huge dark eyes were alive and filled with so much activity that Sabine immediately went to Red Alert trying to access some sort of Universal Translator. There was urgent information being exchanged, but Sabine couldn't quite latch on to it.

Sabine flashed on the time when Freddie Mercury was a tiny kitten, got out into the condo hall and disappeared from the face of the earth.

Inconsolable and distraught, she roamed the halls and street alleyways for two days and two nights, streamers of black mascara stuck to her cheeks with dried tears, her bright red eyes rimmed with melting black eyeliner. She had called in sick to work, which was not an exaggeration, and except for Doctor Crusher and Higgs-Boson needing her she might not have come out of that in one contiguous piece.

On day two she heard Freddie's orotund and angry cries in the basement near the garbage chute. She found him, sitting atop a dead mouse, in one triumphant piece. She had to take another three days off from work to sit in bed and recover.

And there, in the elevator, was a small, emaciated teenage girl wearing a sky blue hospital gown with pictures of clouds and elephants on it. "Oh my God. Here, let me help you." Sabine quickly stepped into the elevator. "Hold on to me."

The door closed and Denize shifted her weight over to Sabine's shoulder. Although Denize still had one hand on the rail, Sabine realized that actually the girl was heavy. Sabine's arrhythmia kicked back in, and she, too, grabbed the railing with her free hand.

"Where are you trying to go?" Sabine whispered. Denize started to slip out of Sabine's grasp. "You can't be running around loose," Sabine said. This was fast becoming an Incident.

"I'm looking for my grandmother," Denize whispered. Her dark skin was turning pale. "Or maybe she was her sister. I found something when my Ancestry DNA came back. It's important. It's a document. I need to get it from her."

Sabine kicked off her right high heel - and since her hands were busy holding up Denize and herself, she used her right foot to hit the red elevator help button. The elevators were brand new, and the old help phones had been replaced with red buttons close to the floor to make them accessible to all sorts of heights in various situations.

What usually happened was that people's kids, who were eye level with the bright red button, would push it. Pushing the button – like most buttons throughout the building – triggered an automatic call to the switchboard. The operator was then responsible for paging maintenance if the elevator was broken, or overhead paging a Rapid Response Code if the person was having an episode of some sort. Or dismissing the call if it was someone's kid pressing buttons.

The month before, there was the issue where the elevator emergency buttons were auto-triggering themselves, and calling the switchboard every eleven minutes for four days straight. Maintenance worked on it, but they fixed the wrong elevator. So the actual elevator company was called in, and a war began between hospital maintenance and Stillwell Elevators, each claiming that the problem was the fault of the other. Finally they decided to alternate repair days, but neither side wanted the button fixed on their day because that would be admitting that they had been the one at fault.

During this mishap, with the emergency button calling the switchboard every eleven minutes, Valentine, Tashuna, and Wing who were on the day shifts then and Sabine, Glo, and Aja who were on the night shifts, kept logs of these calls at the request of Maintenance. Of course each elevator call had to be answered just in case someone was actually stuck in there. So finally Maintenance decided to disconnect the button altogether until the situation was cleared up. Which was great for the operators as it allowed them to answer actual phone calls, page doctors, and announce codes. But of course it meant that when your stockinged foot grappled for the red button while holding up a near-dead teenager and you finally pressed it, nothing happened.

A similar thing happened with the bathrooms across the hall from Telecomm. Some department, no one ever knew which one, installed emergency help buttons that could be activated by someone having a calamitous experience in the bathroom. This button triggered an audible alarm. Unfortunately, the digital part of the alarm was not hooked up – and unless someone passing by in the hall happened to hear the ringing, the luckless soul in the bathroom had to figure out his catastrophe by himself.

In fact, the Trummel Emergency Preparedness Committee had facilitated a hospital-wide button the nurses could push if someone were having a heart attack. Rodney Yates, the head of the committee, wanted to be a hero and save lives, but he was consumed in his private life with his wife selling nonexistent biofuel credits under a federal clean energy program and he forgot to attach the button to anything. So when a patient started seizing and his heart started stopping, the nurse would press this new button with the optimism of a 22nd century *Star Trek* digital healer, and then nothing would happen. Rodney then left the hospital team to raise his children, since his wife was now working eight hours a day spearing trash off the side the Route 95, per order of the Attorney General's office.

So Sabine flashed on a little prayer of urgent hopefulness as she kicked the red emergency button with the side of her stockinged foot, and hoped that help would be on the way. She knew no one wore pantyhose anymore, but you do what you have to do in an emergency. Denize was slipping from her arm and was almost on the floor as *"This is Operator Glo, do you need assistance on the elevator?"* came through the speaker above the button. Tom and the Doo Dah Men had evidently plugged it back in.

"Glo, it's Sabine!" she shouted back. "Um..."

"What's going on, Sabine?" Glo yelled back. Despite the apparently newly repaired technology, Sabine and, it appeared, Glo, were convinced they still had to yell.

"Yes, I seem to be holding a patient up, Glo. A very sick teenage girl with elephants and clouds on her hospital nightgown."

"Alright, stand by, I was just going to announce a Code Amber on her. The nurse on Three called in that our teenager was missing."

You weren't allowed to use people's names over intercoms, overheads, or pagers, because of the Federal privacy rules, but Glo evidently knew who Sabine had found. In hospital work you had to develop your psychic senses, because that was often the only means of coherent communication.

"Where are you?" Glo shouted.

"Somewhere in elevator stack two!"

And then over the loudspeakers, Operator Glo's trained ex-airline flight attendant voice, slightly crackled with time and margaritas, emerged, smooth and calm like a plane making a routine landing: "Attention all personnel. Rapid Response to Elevator L2. Rapid Response to Elevator L2. Thank you. Thank you very much."

When the elevator door finally opened, Sabine and Denize were on the floor in a pool of coagulating crimson, Sabine with a wild look of "It's all under control, I'm a professional," and Denize pretty much passed out. Victor and Eusebio from Security stared back.

"Cool!" said Eusebio.

"What's she doing?" said Victor.

"Duh," said Sabine. "She's looking for her grandmother."

"Okay," said Victor. "We're good. The elevator button seems to be working."

A couple walked up to the elevator banks, animated in an emotional discussion and unaware of the blood and gore, panic and security, pandemonium and chaos. "I can't decide if these are floaties I'm seeing or if there are gnats circling my head," one was saying. "It would be better if they were floaties," the other answered. "It would be better if they were gnats," the first one retorted angrily.

Chapter 5

After Talking Heads came out with Life During Wartime (this Ain't No Disco), Sabine realized it wasn't just her. She was actually on to something.

"I've seen enough *Twilight Zone* to know when I'm being contacted from another dimension," Sabine said to Juliet as they took shelter from the damp cold at the Black Cat Lounge. The women sat down at a small round table by the bay window in the front, and peeled off their coats and scarves.

"I'm keeping my gloves on," Juliet answered. "I'm chilled to the bone."

"When I met Denize in the elevator - Juliet, you should have been there. We totally connected. I didn't know who she was, but I knew it was her. There was a recognition on both our parts. Is the wine here yet?"

Juliet looked around the dimly lit, amber room to see if there was anything to verify Sabine's expectation of wine arriving quickly. On the walls were framed yellowing photos of historic Trummel – unsmiling mustached men with suspenders and caps, standing in front of old brick textile mills. Then she took a gold Estée Lauder compact from her clutch and popped it open. She inspected her beige satin lipstick to make sure it had made it intact through the short car ride from their condo to the Black Cat. Her creamy, poreless complexion also made it through the late autumn slosh, and her hair, which today tumbled in loose curls around her shoulders, was smooth and golden, like a movie star. "You had a recognition," Juliet said, turning the tiny mirror slightly to check a shadow under the right side of her jaw. "It's a moment. An occurrence."

"Thank God," Sabine said. She leaned in to look at the menu, making the table wobble. "It felt like when my eyes met Denize, some information was being, well, I don't want to say transmitted, but let's just say communicated. I don't know why."

Juliet snapped her compact shut and her eyes lit up as if from an internal heat source. "My dear neighbor, it was supersymmetry, there's no doubt about it. It happens all the time, we just don't usually notice it because, you know, these are tiny particles we're talking about."

"My elevator meeting with Denize was supersymmetry?"

"Not the meeting, Sabine. The connection that you guys made. Particles from different dimensions acting in consort, like they're married. Or well, okay, but you have a particle in dimension A, say, and millions of light years and ten dimensions away its partner particle knows exactly what's up with it. Like twins. Particle A shimmies to the left and its mate, Particle B in dimension X, shimmies to the right. At exactly the same time. They're connected. And then when we get that sorted out, we'll go to New York. We'll party in nightclubs. It will be fabulous."

Sabine paused momentarily to adjust to Juliet's new take on things. "We're middle-aged."

"Oh who cares. Where's the wine list?"

"You're married."

"He can come with us." Juliet sighed, and her mood dropped slightly. "Wine list?"

"I have the wine list memorized. There's red and there's white."

"You're upset."

"Just on a day to day thing," Sabine explained. "I'm not upset about the big picture because I don't get it. It's clear that you have a handle on it, though, Juliet, and for that I'm grateful. Someone has to have a handle on something, right? But it turns out Human Resources put in their files that I was in an Incident. They created an Incident Report."

"For helping a lost patient in the elevator?"

"Yes. I stepped on to the elevator and there was Denize, and I said Let me help you, and then it became an Incident. That's how these things develop. Once you have an Incident it's downhill from there. Everyone hates you and then you get laid off. I have no other income, not since my ex invested in this start-up company that was designing a catapult for a projectile to impede incoming meteors. And I can't stand not being liked, it's a survival thing."

Words like *event*, *incident*, and *episode* were popular hospital HR designations for unpleasant occurrences, because of their exquisitely precise generalities. They implied importance while remaining opaque. They notified higher up file readers that something occurred, without giving any information.

"I'm all too familiar with Incidents, Sabine."

Sabine relaxed a little. "I'm glad to hear it." She felt validated that Juliet knew what she was talking about. She flashed on how fabulous it was to have a friend who was worldly. Who understood nuances. Who knew the ramifications of having one's name in some file. Who could put it into perspective.

The Black Cat was in the middle of Main Street. A low glow came from small table lights and wall sconces, giving it a city neighborhood feel. Outside it was already dark at 4:30 p.m., but the funeral home next door and the accordion repair shop across the street lit up the pedestrians passing by. Even though Trummel had a population of at least five thousand, the

Black Cat was never more than half full. Sabine couldn't figure out where everyone went at night. A gentle sleeting rain was hitting the big picture window and cars made a dampened slushing sound outside.

A heavy-set woman with jet black hair and deep eye bags over pale skin came to the little table. "Yes ladies?" She co-owned the place, with her husband. Without waiting for an answer she turned and shouted at a young boy who was sitting at the bar with his notebooks scattered about. "Finish your math, Frederic." She had what Sabine thought might be a Russian accent, at least that's the accent they used on Law and Order Criminal Intent when they had the episodes with Russian characters. She briefly flashed on her ongoing crush with Vincent D'Onofrio, but only the episodes before the beard and the episode with the psychiatric hospital.

The heavy-set woman turned back to Juliet and Sabine. "What can I get you?"

Juliet looked up at her and smiled into the distance. "You know, Karina, I was just thinking how lovely it would be to enjoy a velvety glass of Beaujolais Nouveau."

Karina breathed deeply and continued to wait, her expression completely unchanged, as if Juliet hadn't yet spoken.

"House red," Juliet said.

Karina looked to Sabine.

"Yes, red for me too."

She turned and left.

"Okay, look," Sabine whispered across the table. "Just like you said, there's a deeper message in my serendipitous meeting with Denize. I don't know what it is, but I know it's there. Something I'm not seeing. We made eye contact and there was a recognition."

"Well we'll just have to get to the bottom of it. Okay, it's finally warming up in here." She peeled off her cashmere gloves and laid them carefully on the table.

In a town where the norm was missing teeth, chronic back pain, and hepatitis B, one might think that Juliet would stand out as eccentric. But the Trummel crowd, filtering along Main Street and through the Black Cat, had more important things going on. The shooting at the hospital, most recently. Then the intrigue of a hospital operator lying in a pool of coagulated blood on an elevator floor with the recovering shooting victim.

More compelling were the rumors flying around town. When rumors flew around the hospital they were by definition flying around the town, since everyone in town was a frequent flyer at the hospital. The town-hospital unit was a closed, self-contained, self-sustaining ecosystem of people cycling from their livingrooms into an ambulance, through the Emergency Room, and into a hospital bed. From there they filtered into the Operating Room, then back to their livingroom, and finally back into the Emergency Room for re-admittance into the hospital with the next infection. Like a mobius strip.

Nyx and the other information officers had realized, in putting together a systems flow chart, and of course Nyx's flow charts were all verbal which prevented the misunderstandings that so often occurred with paper and digital mediums – not to mention computers were seldom available to the information staff which mainly depended on germ-zapping floor polishers for its hardware - that Sabine's bloody encounter with Denize in the elevator was an important departure from the Trummel cycle of life.

So as the information officers dispersed from their headquarters in the second floor linen closet, they made all departments – not the department heads, of course, but rather the regular healthcare workers, from nurses to food service staff, to Telecommunications, to transcription, to medical coding, to x-ray tech - aware that there had been an Incident. This was over and above HR's official Incident Report. It had more details and a more humanistic approach.

Attached to this verbal Incident Report were theories about why Denize would be running around the hospital half-dead. These theories were based on fact, of course. The fact was something about Denize's rants concerning her missing grandmother when she was first admitted and had became delirious with a high fever. And, too, from that first night, information had been distributed about the shooter, Clea, also frantic about a missing document, this one from overseas, and the fact that Clea had been wearing fleece-lined wafflestompers during her shooting spree. That was information. A clue.

No one had heard from Clea since Victor had carried her heroically, like a first responder, to the Psych Unit that night. She had been distraught, and access to the PUF, or Program Unit Facility as the psych unit was called, was limited to staff and patients only. PUF even had their own information staff, none of whom shared anything, but Nyx was taking classes toward getting certified for work there, and it was only a matter of weeks until she got her clearance.

The wine came. Karina plopped the two glasses onto the table, and zipped away yelling "Just Google it, Frederic!" towards the bar. "Two plus two equals twenty-two, last time I checked."

Sabine grabbed her wine glass stem to make sure nothing spilled as the table wobbled.

Juliet looked at her wine and sighed in deep relief at its arrival. Nothing actually showed on her face, but it was something Sabine picked up on. Things relating to wine interested her deeply.

"Should you be drinking?" Sabine said, hoping Juliet would say yes of course she should be drinking. Sabine had just found a new friend. It would be devastating if Juliet actually did have some medical issue and wouldn't be able to drink. Sabine hoped that maybe Juliet had fainted and ended up in the emergency room simply due to stress, perhaps, or better yet a reaction from her Vietnam PTSD, or maybe an overwhelm of some sort.

"I'm hydrating." Juliet smiled. "So - what actually happened when you met Denize in the elevator?"

"I mean, okay, here's what happened. Before I pushed the elevator help button with my foot, the nurse on Three noticed Denize missing and called Glo at the switchboard to announce a Code Gray. She told Glo she thought Denize ran down stairway six. Glo announced over the loudspeakers about the Code Gray in stairway six. No one knew where stairway six was. And of course the code should have been a Code Amber. And it was elevator two, not stairway six. So even after I pushed the help button with my foot, it took Security a while to get there. I had more time with Denize. We almost spoke."

Juliet took a sip of her wine. "You realize that this whole thing is a mass hallucination, right? The problem is we're all stuck in it. That's the issue. There's your Incident, right there."

With a deep breath and an almost ah-ha smile, Sabine tilted her head as if juggling that idea around to see if it fit anywhere. Maybe Juliet was on to something. It was worth keeping an open mind, since Juliet was thin and it was unclear what she did for a living.

Here was the thing: Sabine thought that if Juliet's cool presence could rub off on her, she'd be one step closer to sanity. As it was, Sabine often felt she was a mere breath away from panic at all times. The feeling of panic was so constant that it would have been her default state of consciousness had it not been for her training as a hospital operator. Repressed panic was what being alive felt like. Unchecked, the nightmares about losing her cats, about her roof caving in, about inter-dimensional insect invasions, about war planes filling the sky and fire balls crashing to earth, ran rampant.

That was why Sabine stayed in Trummel – she had a job in a place that functioned within the undertow of being completely unglued, and she got to be in daily contact with people who understood the concept of losing it completely. People who were all just one dark thought away from frothing oblivion. With imminent meltdowns just beneath the surface, triggered by thoughts of babies being thrown to American soldiers on helicopters as Saigon was falling; by someone's beloved child who grew up to be a Delta Force soldier in Somalia, murdered when his Black Hawk went down; of Thomas Edison electrocuting an elephant in Manhattan.

Sabine was comfortable amidst people who spontaneously burst their spleens or chopped off their toes. People who popped things. Who couldn't remember where they were. Trummel was safe. A safe place.

Sabine's flourishing new friendship with Juliet was enabling her to reverse engineer some of this panic methodology. Juliet had every reason to fall on the floor in drooling seizures. She had PTSD, she had been in a war-zone which she wouldn't talk about, she lived in Trummel, gorgeous and unacknowledged. She had a husband who was never home. But she projected Paris. She wore Chanel, smiled about inward murmurings from other universes, and could wear perfume without people around her sneezing. Juliet always said everything was okay. Who's to say she wasn't right, Sabine thought. The Universe is huge – a hundred billion galaxies according to Neil deGrasse

Tyson, Carl Sagan's spiritual doppelganger. Multiplied exponentially if you count the extra eleven dimensions in the String Theory's Multiverse, this pointed to a quantum uncertainty. Who's to know what's actually going on? Certainly not HR, for godssake.

"Alright, so look. I'm putting two things together here," said Sabine. "First, Clea said she shot Denize because Denize had some information and wouldn't share. Now Denize says she has to get some urgent papers from her grandmother."

Juliet gazed across the small table at Sabine. "I am a grandmother. Did I ever tell you?"

Sabine tried to use her well-developed alchemy skills to transform the grizzly ice she saw out the window into a feeling of being inside a warm, golden gathering spot. She knew warm and golden, they were her goals in life. But like those dreams where you're trying to scream and no sound comes out – or you're trying to call 911 and the line is dead – she was never able to actually get there.

"You never told me you were a grandmother, Juliet. I assumed you had some family somewhere, but I didn't want to pry."

Juliet smiled. "Yes. And I have a daughter, Linette. She's an architect. She works for a firm in Budapest."

"Do you get to see her?"

"Oh yes. When I'm … in Budapest."

"Does she get to the states?"

"Absolutely, Sabine. You'll meet her I'm sure."

Sabine, too, had family, but they were mostly exes and deceased. "I'm trying to make my life feel like it's continuously meaningful. As opposed to intermittently tolerable. The ups and downs are too unpredictable to be counted on."

"Well, I mean if you want unpredictable, there's the continuous threat of annihilation by anti-matter," Juliet said with a scholarly lift of her perfectly plucked left eyebrow.

"Annihilation by anti-matter," Sabine mused, and sipped her wine. "You say that like it's a bad thing."

"Well, if it's not painful."

"I see your point."

At a table near the restrooms, two ladies were arguing. "I have a wheelchair, a walker, and a cane," bragged the first one. "I have a wheelchair, two walkers, and six canes," said the other with a smug smile.

That's when Raphael came over from the bar. "Can I join you?" He was about forty-five, a mere child, Sabine thought. He wore jeans and a heavy cable-knit sweater with a neatly pressed shirt collar coming out of the top. His hair was dark and thick, but nicely cut, and his slight five o'clock shadow was unaffected, not intentional. "You're Sabine from the hospital, right?"

Sabine sighed as he plopped his beer down and made everyone's drinks wobble. She had left her badge on.

"I'm Raphael." He pulled over a wooden chair from the empty next table and sat down. Juliet watched him with a detached interest.

"Your voice sounds familiar," Sabine said. "I'm into voices."

"Yep." He smiled. "I'm the guy from the *Sun* who you wouldn't talk to."

"Oh, you're a real person."

"That I am, my dear controlling switchboard operator."

Sabine studied him. He wasn't wearing scrubs or a toolbelt, and his voice wasn't coming through a police scanner, so she didn't immediately know how to place him in the hierarchy of male presences. "I guess we were pretty awful to you on the phone."

"Not your fault, Sabine. I know all about medical privacy. I was just working my angle." He turned to Juliet and his smile broadened, as if expecting her to introduce herself. She gazed back.

Federal and state privacy laws loomed over all healthcare workers. The laws were constantly being updated and revised, and few people knew exactly what not to say to whom. This was why no one told anyone anything. Being paranoid was being smart. All one had to do to not mess up was to keep your mouth closed, and make sure you faxed your patient's lab results to the correct doctor's office and not to the morgue by mistake. The fact that any department knew what another department was doing, even to the same patient, happened through pure synchronicity.

Raphael was engrossed in smiling at Juliet.

"Um, Raphael, this is my friend Juliet," Sabine said, hoping to nip an existential moment in the bud. She had seen people fall into Juliet's gaze and have trouble climbing out. She seemed to remember even Clea the shooter seeming more gentle with Juliet in the room.

Raphael took Juliet's hand. He stopped short of kissing it. "Hello, Juliet."

"Hello Raphael." Juliet pulled her hand back firmly but gently. "Did the switchboard ladies abuse you?"

"Why yes. Yes they did."

"Hey, that's enough self-pity," Sabine said. "I put you through to Glo who put you through to Barbara Vermouth. The rest is up to you."

He sighed, took up his beer mug, and turned to Sabine. "And the universe."

Sabine unclipped the badge from the collar of her soft blue sweater and tucked it into the purse on her lap. She quickly ran her hands through her long brown hair and over her straight bangs. "I just put the calls through, I have no control of who doesn't answer."

"Oh don't worry about it, Sabine. I'm just giving you a hard time."

Raphael was pale as a zombie, underneath a thin layer of dark, Mediterranean skin - and that together with his bloodshot eyes and emaciated body made him fit in quite well with everyone else in Trummel who got no sunlight for most of the year and who lived on frozen fish sticks and white bread. Sabine figured Raphael would be mobile for maybe another ten years, and then he'd slip seamlessly into the hospital ecosystem.

Trummel was a trauma hospital, meaning that the emergency room was the hot spot for car accidents, bee bite anaphylaxis, assault victims, accidental overdoses, and other assorted disasters the EMTs brought in. But if it was something huge, like a broken pacemaker or a Delta Level breathing issue, or an attempted hanging, Lulu from the ER would call Sabine on the Dispatch line and have her arrange for an ambulance or helicopter to rush them to Manhattan so the Trummel team wouldn't kill them.

Which was another puzzling fact about Denize Leclair.

"What I'm wondering, though," asked Raphael, "is how come you guys didn't airlift the teenager out. I mean, a through and through gunshot wound?"

"Sorry, Raphael." Sabine sipped her wine. "You're going to get me fired, isn't there something else you could write about?"

"Honestly, not that much, Sabine."

Raphael, Sabine, and Juliet sat close together at the little round table and stared out the window onto Main Street in Zen-like contemplation.

"I'm trying to think of other things you can write about," said Juliet. "There must be secrets buried in a Victorian garden gone to pot somewhere that you could dig up."

"Thank you, Juliet," said Raphael. "I sense that you are an empath."

Juliet turned and actually looked at Raphael. "Few people understand that."

Raphael smiled back. "It's a burden. I know."

Juliet looked down at the table, as if the connection was just a little too strong too soon. She took a sip of wine, leaving lipstick on the rim. "Knowing things, Raphael. It's not so much a burden, it's just that when you know stuff, then people at large can't relate to you. Wait, no. It's me who can't relate to them."

Raphael put on a Hey-I've-Been-There look, which would have gone well with a loosened tie had he been wearing one.

"Oh for God's sake," Sabine said. "Hello." She picked up her wine. "Earth to Alpha Centauri."

Raphael laughed and turned to Sabine. For an instant Sabine felt a remnant of what he had been shooting at Juliet. An intense, probing look, a quick departure from anything day to day, a glimpse into something subterranean that Sabine knew she knew, but couldn't put a finger on. Like a vivid dream that stays with you all the next day, even though you can't remember it.

Sabine felt her circuits overload a little. She went back to what was safe. "So we sent your call to Barbara Vermouth, our public relations person. She is actually allowed to tell you stuff for the paper. Didn't she update you on Denize Leclair's condition?"

"Oh I suppose so, but it was mostly that Denize was still in serious condition. I heard over my police scanner that there was a code in the elevator, and I know it's got something to do with it, but I'm here on the outside, looking in. This is driving me to certain extinction. I used to live in the East Village. I ran a free newspaper. I saw *The Ravenous Ombudsmen* at

CBGB's in 1987 and wrote a review about them for *Rolling Stone.*

Juliet turned to Raphael. "I was walking down the street last week and then suddenly I woke up in the ER."

"You see?" Raphael flashed a smile of it's-a-small-world recognition. "Exactly!" He held out his hand for Juliet to high-five, but Juliet was not on the high-five wavelength.

"Give it here," Sabine said, and held up her hand to make sure his high-five didn't go unrequited. She thought of her three ragamuffin cats. Raphael didn't respond. The whole thing collapsed.

"Hey, Sabine," Raphael said. "What's up with you and Denize Leclair in a pool of blood in the elevator today? Were you, like, attempting a double suicide or what?"

"Oh for godssake," Sabine said. "Deal with it. And get us another round, okay?"

"Actually, I think I have to get back to the condo," Juliet said, glancing at her empty wrist. "*Through the Wormhole with Morgan Freeman* is on and he discusses the Shadow Biosphere. This is important information."

Sabine and Raphael looked to Juliet, waiting for further Intel. After a few moments of nothing forthcoming, Raphael's eyes gleamed and a hint of a genuine smile crossed his face and then disappeared.

"You... are into the Shadow Biosphere?" he said. His voice took on a lower, intimate tone.

Sabine caught Raphael's look and stood up, bumping the table. "Come on, then, Juliet, we'd better hurry."

Juliet looked at Raphael. "Why yes. You too?"

"Of course," he said.

Sabine's panic default mode was starting to kick in. She couldn't put it into words, but she suddenly felt creeped out.

"The rock from Mars," Juliet continued. "The ASH84001 – contained trapped atmospheric gasses. I've seen this episode a few times."

Raphael turned slowly to Sabine. "You go ahead, Sabine. You can tape it for her. Me and Juliet have some things to talk about."

Sabine swung her scarf around her neck and put her gloves on. "I don't have a taping component." She waited, trying to figure out what to do next. And then she realized, as she waited, that although she looked to Juliet for her other-worldly wisdom, this wisdom was fragile. Or perhaps Juliet was fragile. Or maybe they both were. A plan still hadn't come to her. And Juliet had a husband somewhere.

But thankfully, Juliet stood up, taking her white wool coat off her chair and slipping it on. "You're young yet," she said to Raphael. "Will you pick up the check?"

"You bet," he said, as if nothing had passed between them. Or at least as if nothing had gone through his own head.

"Leave a good tip, okay?" Juliet added as she and Sabine headed for the door.

"I will leave a good tip."

"Alright then," said Sabine. "We'll all pray for a good outcome."

"I'm just glad you got into and out of the emergency room in one piece." Raphael sat back in his chair as if Juliet's leaving did not affect his life. "I figure if you can wake up in the ER in the middle of the night, you being a goddess, how are the rest of us normal slobs expected to cope, you know?"

As the women ran shivering to Sabine's VW in the Black Cat parking lot, they passed two guys going the other way. One said, "I want alcoholics. I want various survivors. I want old and young…" .

Chapter 6

Sabine's need to prepare for the annihilation of earth, which wouldn't be a problem if it didn't involve her cats, was informed in her early years - when television was first invented - by Flash Gordon defying Emperor Ming the Merciless. Ming was about to smash their two planets together.

And then in her middle years, there was Schrödinger's cat, which upset her greatly.

Even during the annual east coast fall-into-winter metastasis, Sabine kept spring in mind, and visualized it dripping daily into her cellular system like the saline drips everyone had in the emergency room. The movement of the seasons gave her the momentum she needed to bolster the constantly approaching cosmic entropy - or was the entropy in her own mind, projected outward to give the impression that it was the cosmos that was falling apart, not her - by working constantly to maintain an attitude of radical nonresistance, inspired by having recently read Eckhart Tolle's **The Power of Now**.

The skills that resulted in Sabine's coping cache were reinforced by her new friendship with Juliet, who was reading Ray Kurzweil's *The Singularity is Near*. This logically led Sabine to the feeling of groundlessness defined by Pema Chodron. Actually Pema said "positive" groundlessness, but Sabine couldn't go that far, it was too extreme. She could do groundless and still feel that her cats were safe.

Driving to the hospital in her VW bug that evening, Sabine listened to her Sly & the Family Stone Pandora channel playing *There's a Riot Goin' On*. She was loyal to her generation – a vast spectrum of diverse beats. She respected Aja's generation's music, although she preferred to call it pop culture, but the feeling was, if it gets you through the night, just let it be. It's fine. Leave it alone.

Sabine opened her car windows for a second, to take in the fresh winter air. She closed them before the pelting gray sleet triggered a memory of her childhood cat, Particle, who was kidnapped by some guy who broke into her family home one night.

Sometimes on her drive to work she remembered things from long ago, hazy things that she couldn't completely verbalize. These flashes of memory-remnants were deeply intriguing, and hinted at why she had chosen to come to earth at this particular time and in this particular situation. With all the dimensions that might have been possible, some perhaps filled only with golden suns shining on green lawns blanketed with lounging long-haired cats, there must have been a reason she chose Trummel. It was safe, she thought. But there was some information missing.

She knew that Juliet knew something, although neither knew what it was. But Juliet's searches were more solid. Juliet hadn't heard from her daughter in Budapest in quite some time and didn't have the cash to go over there and check on her. Deepak Chopra had released a video saying that one's real self, one's inner "you", actually had no location in space/time. Juliet felt she could utilize that information to check on Linette, but was waiting for further Intel.

Sabine clicked on her left turn signal even though no one else was on the road, and drove into the Emergency Room lot. She parked in the employee row, a short walk from the door. There was something about Denize Leclair.

Sabine had taken to visiting the teenager as she was recovering at Trummel Rehab, down the street. Denize had been undergoing intensive physical therapy to get walking again, and she was taking all sorts of meds to keep food down and infection away. But more important, Denize contained information that was at the core of Sabine's unknown quest. And that had been amplified by the hysteria of the Code Amber.

Clea, the teenage attempted murderer, was still upstairs in PUF, the psych unit. No one could get up there to see her except strangers with briefcases. Even Raphael, the investigative journalist, was unable to get information about Clea. To keep himself employed, he had taken to writing *Sun* articles about pre-migraine hallucinations and strangely behaving subatomic particles. He had evidently been brainstorming with Juliet. Nyx was working toward getting into PUF, but had not yet finished the required course work.

Every year, each employee had to complete a series of online courses. They mostly had to do with hand-washing and how not to spread super-bugs through the patient rooms, how to not irradiate yourself walking through Nuclear Med to deliver a phone message because they never pick up their phones, and of course the big one - how to not get yourself fired or thrown in jail for sharing information. Yes, the dreaded and sacred HIPAA doctrine.

It was just a year ago that Baibin from the lab was in the elevator with Alfonso Brown and Sister Sadie from the local diocese who were there to give last rites to a renal failure patient. He was telling them about the recent encounter with necrotizing fasciitis, the flesh-eating thing that Lulu found on someone who came in through the emergency room. Victor from Security happened to be listening in on the elevator's transmitter, and reported the information breach to admin. Baibin from the lab was never seen again.

Sabine parked the VW bug in a fabulous space right by the Emergency Room door, stopped in the cafeteria for coffee, and took the elevator down to LL2, the official independent network of cave dwellers. The Telecomm operators kept doctors connected to blood test results, and patients connected to doctors. Even though the hospital staff and admin had no knowledge of their existence, Sabine, Glo and Aja - and the three alternate operators Valentine, Tashuna, and Wing - stayed spiritually relevant knowing that they were the connecting force of the hospital and the hospital was the hub of the town.

This gave Sabine enough spurts of flailing self-esteem to keep the possibility of male companionship on her to-do list, even if it was scheduled for a time in the future when she'd have it all pulled together. It would have to be a man who loved animals. Maybe an independent film buff or a PBS supporter. He would have to like wine. Some sort of passion.

"Thank you for calling Trummel Hospital, this is Operator Glo, how can I help you?" Sabine heard as she walked into the switchboard room with three cups of steaming coffee balanced in a cardboard tray.

The Keurig had died, and its corpse lay in the corner behind the engineer's desk. It had become another surface on which to affix post-its. *Do not announce Helicopters after 7:30pm, because patients Might be sleeping*, said one, and *Do Not overhead page Dr. Ythanipcvlevilli,* said another.

Adding to the switchboard room's dark, richly textured wall decor were peeling decals of fading Christmas trees, Halloween pumpkins, bunnies romping with daisies in their mouths - and shriveling bulletin board notes regarding the Dr. Mu Fui issue. She was an ER physician, but no one knew if it was Dr. Mu Fui or Dr. Fui Mu, and she never answered her beeper page. In person everyone just called her Doctor. Glo had her in the Telecomm data base twice, once under each name. Even IT didn't know.

Henry Moho, whom everyone assumed was an IT administrator of some importance because he wore a suit and was only seen walking quickly through the halls, didn't know. Sabine had asked him once, stopping him as he raced by. She couldn't stop by his office, because no one knew where that was. His hospital extension wasn't listed in her computer database. When he called through the switchboard his extension showed up as *Inner Core RYB0720,* but calling back to 0720 just got a fast busy signal. Henry once told Sabine in the hall that there was no way to fix the Issue regarding Dr. Mu Fui because the data entry clerk who had typed in her name had had a psychotic break and could not be reached.

The other problem with trying to identify Henry Moho's department, Sabine knew, was that Henry never carried anything identifiable as he walked quickly through the halls. Doctors and nurses had stethoscopes slung around their necks. Lab techs carried trays of biohazards and needles. Social workers carried overstuffed day planners, rubber bands around their wrists, and phone numbers on scrap paper falling from their totes. Phlebotomists pushed around trays with blood in test tubes. It was all orderly.

Sabine put a coffee down in front of Aja.

"I'm sorry, Sir," Aja was saying into her headset, "I can't put you through to her room. Yes I know she's your girlfriend, but you still need to know her name." Aja looked up at Sabine and nodded a thank you as she gently pried the lid off the cup.

Sabine put Glo's coffee down and then sat at her own station, between Aja and Glo. She slid her headset on, trying not to ruin her blowout or catch her small gold hoop earrings.

"Thank you for calling Trummel Hospital, this is Sabine, how can I help you?"

"I'm looking for a patient by the name of French," Sabine's caller said.

Sabine checked the census on her computer screen for that name. "I don't have that patient listed."

"It's French," the caller insisted. *"Spelled T-H-O-M-A-S."*

"Oh. Thomas French?"

"No. Thomas. T-H-O-M-A-S. He's French."

"Oh. I'm so sorry, Sir, he's still not here. I totally apologize." Sabine clicked EndCall.

"Sabine." Aja put a hand over her microphone and turned. "Enter the frozen yogurt contest in the cafeteria today and win a free autopsy."

"Okay," Sabine said. "Are you guys entering?"

"Yes, we're both in," said Glo.

"Hey, by the way, Sabine," Aja said. Her youth and maxi skirt belied her credibility, and she knew it, so to compensate she went into her professional local news anchor voice. "We're not using Merit's ambulances until further notice. Somebody fell off a stretcher."

Operator Glo snorted in acknowledgment, somewhere between contempt and amusement, not looking up from her computer. "Yeah, like Valley Ambulance never dropped anyone," she said. "Thank you for calling Trummel – no, pneumococcal starts with a 'p'. Yes I'm sure. You're welcome."

At that moment, Henry Moho appeared in the hall, walking fast and carrying something - a stack of paper files. His suit was wrinkled, which ruled out lawyer, trustee, or funeral director. IT people didn't wear suits. Risk management? Sabine, Aja, and Glo, who had hashed out this issue repeatedly over many years, had decided that he was some sort of cyber security person. Or maybe Linens. The problem was he always got his lunch to go, so no one ever saw who he ate with. And yes he did wear a badge, but it dangled from a lariat, permanently backward. Sabine thought maybe his badge was backward on both sides, like a fixed deck. He could be a government agent.

"He could be the anti-Christ," Glo had recently reflected. "We just don't know."

"Henry!" Sabine called as she saw him. She knew her window of opportunity to get Intel from him was quick and narrow. She ran into the hall to intercept him.

He stopped, almost toppling forward from the shift in momentum. He turned around and squinted at Sabine's badge. "Sabine."

"Who do I talk to about the nurses calling the wrong code names down to the switchboard?"

Henry was heavyset, with grayish brown hair that was perhaps a day overdo for a shampoo. He didn't change expression or acknowledge comprehension, but just waited.

"Last week?" Sabine said. "When one of the patients got lost? The nurse called down to Telecomm to announce a Code Gray, but it should have been a Code Amber. Code Amber is a lost patient. When they say the wrong code, then the wrong people come to help. I've been working on getting this fixed for forever."

A hint of puzzlement flew across Henry's face, hitting one eye first and then the other, like a fast moving train.

"Is there some way we can get everyone on the same page?" Sabine continued. "Like, I don't know, a manual or a P&P? I was in the elevator with the lost patient and she was in really bad shape, and it took them a while to find us because the elevators and stairwells are not labeled. Can we somehow get a way to label the stairwells and elevators so missing patients can be found?"

"You were the one who found our lost patient?" Henry said.

"Yes."

"Good work, Sabine."

"Oh. Thank you. But I'm not a nurse. All I could do was keep her company until the Rapid Response team arrived."

"So our elevator help button protocol went smoothly then."

"The button did work, Henry, yes."

"Excellent. Thank you for being a team player, Sabine." He turned to go.

"So can I requisition Facilities to put up signage on the stairwells and elevators?"

He stopped and turned again, keeping a lean into his forward momentum so as not to lose time getting up to speed when this was over.

"And maybe get a memo out reminding everyone what color goes with what disaster?" Sabine put it all out there. There was no telling when someone with authority might be down in the second lower level again.

"We can do a requisition," Henry said.

"Okay, good. Thank you."

"You are welcome, my dear."

"But I need someone to sign it. Can you sign the form right now and I'll fill it out after?"

Henry sighed as if now totally tired of this basement diversion. "What department are you in, Sabine?"

"Telecomm."

"We still have a Telecomm department?"

"Henry, you're standing right in front of it. It's the switchboard, the overhead announcements, and dispatch."

"We were hiring a consulting firm to implement an automated system to replace Telecomm, Sabine."

Pick your fights, thought Sabine quickly. "Well, but can you still sign a requisition?"

"Yes, absolutely. Let me catch you later, though, we have a situation on the fourth floor." He lurched forward but suddenly stopped and turned again to Sabine. "By the way, here are those files." He held out the stack of manila folders he had been hugging. Sabine took the files, still warm from his chest, and Henry was off, fading down the hall back into non-existence.

As Sabine walked back into the switchboard room, she flipped through the three-inch thick stack of files. They were filled with loose papers, fold-out charts, project planners, and memos. Glo and Aja had their information radar beams on high. InfoDar, Aja had called it.

"Oh my God," Glo said, licking her lips as if Sabine had an armful of chocolate cake with buttercream frosting. "Information."

"What's in it?" Aja asked.

"No idea." Sabine sat down at her station and spread the files out. The tabs were all written by hand, labeled with unknown abbreviations. In the files were color coded charts of random numbers in columns, project planning forms, and journal entries of unknown origin with indecipherable codes.

"Safe to say we haven't hit the Rosetta Stone for stairwell numbering requisition forms," Glo said.

"Look at this." Sabine pointed to the letters LIBAD, which appeared in the upper right corner of each page.

"Uh-huh," Aja said. "On the plus side, though, if someone calls the switchboard asking to be connected to LIBAD, we now know there is actually such a thing."

"Good point," agreed Sabine. She clicked through some files on her computer. "But nothing saying LIBAD comes up. Where would we send the caller to?"

"Maybe it stands for Leptospirosis in Bacterial Dysmorphia," Glo said. "Someone had that last week. I sent them to Anjelica Cloud in Infection Control."

"It couldn't be that easy," Aja said. "How about Lyme Infection By Alternate Diagnosis. I sent that one to Lulu just yesterday. She thought it was fabulous."

Sabine realized no one was answering the phones, and put her headset on. "Thank you for - Yes, this is the switchboard. Code Blue in the ICU, yes Doctor, right away." She grabbed the microphone that lived between her and Glo, clicked on her computer to activate the overhead, and paged "Attention all personnel. Code Blue in the ICU. Code Blue in the ICU." Sabine wished it didn't rhyme.

Denize Leclair's color was looking less and less lavender every day. Her stomach had been more affected by the bullet than her spine, but she still had pain when trying to walk. Sabine and Glo had brought her magazines and movies when she was first transferred to Trummel Rehab, but today they thought they'd surprise her with something known for its magical healing properties.

"Slippery elm, I hope?" Aja had asked, as Sabine and Glo packed up their totes to leave the nightshift. Aja would stay another hour, and then Valentine, Tashuna, and Wing would stagger shifts throughout the day into the next evening. "Slippery elm is calming, my mom used to give it to me. Or you could bring her Balm of Gilead oil, for pain. I got some online. Just don't eat it. You massage it in."

"I'm not massaging anyone, anytime, any place," Glo huffed. "I don't want to end up with three teenagers again."

Sabine laughed as she tucked her cell phone into her purse. "I'm going to leave that to you, Aja. We have something better. A proven cure. Carvel soft ice cream."

"Besides," Glo added. "This is a hospital, not a freaking health food store." She looked to Sabine for confirmation.

"She can't eat Carvel," Aja said. "Her stomach is barely working."

"That's okay, we'll eat it," Glo said.

Aja turned to her computer. "Thank you for calling Trummel Hospital, this is Aja, how may I help you?"

"Aja doesn't visit her," Glo said to Sabine. "Why do we?"

"Denize doesn't have any family," Sabine said.

"So?"

"This isn't the jail," Aja said into her headset mike. "This is the hospital. To get your son out of jail, you need to call the jail."

"We visit Denize because she was here in our hospital and now she's in rehab," Sabine said.

"You visit Denize," said Glo. "I go with you because you don't want to go by yourself."

"I'm sure your son is a good person, Mrs. Ambrosio," Aja was saying, "and jail must be horrible, but... oh, prison? I think that's different than jail... For life?"

"And you love your Carvel," Sabine said. She and Glo picked up their pink and black purses and their matching totes from the latest 31 party.

As Aja said "Mrs. Ambrosio, I totally have to go, my switchboard is lighting up," Sabine pantomimed a good-by wave to her, and Glo ran an exaggerated invisible knife across her throat, presumably to tell Aja to hang up on Mrs. Ambrosio who called every few days and had spoken to each of the operators a number of times.

Aja was the official softy of the bunch and pickled herself in other people's horrors at least once a day. Last week she took a call from a post-surgical patient recovering in the ICU who had just called 911 to tell them the CIA was trying to kill her.

"The CIA protects us," Aja had said, trying to reassure the patient, who was post-op from a urethroplasty.

"*No my dear,*" the patient said. "*You don't understand. The CIA is after me.*"

Aja paused and then said "Oh, *that* CIA."

But Sabine knew she was much deeper into the empathy spectrum than Aja. Aja felt for others and sometimes put a hand over her heart when describing an Incident. Sabine kept her position on the spectrum her own secret, even from Juliet, even while drinking Merlot on Juliet's balcony with the Eurythmics' *Sweet Dreams* pulsing in the background, and people's porch lights coming on. "For some reason I *am* the cow that is next in line at the slaughterhouse," Sabine had once said to a therapist. "I need to figure this out. I'm worse than Aja."

"No, I don't have the number for the prison," Aja said sweetly.

"Aja, for Godsake." Glo couldn't help herself. "You're going to miss the normal people calling, and that bodes ill for Telecomm. If someone complains about us, then admin might remember that we're here."

Even if Henry's people were planning to extinguish the Telecomm Department, they certainly would never actually get around to it. And of course the operators could always go rogue, since they were pretty much there anyway. Telecomm operators made their own rules. No one knew the difference. The operators paged the codes overhead - no one knew where the pages originated, they were just part of the hospital's background noise.

Aja put Mrs. Ambrosio on mute. "Today is different, Glo," she said. "The poor woman is really out of it, slurring her words. What should I do?"

"Give her to Lulu in the ER," said Sabine. "Maybe there really is something wrong with her."

"Lulu's going to kill me," said Aja. "Yesterday I sent her a caller who had a tick in her head."

"Lulu's a trained trauma nurse," Glo said. "We are, um…"

"We're trained, um…" said Sabine.

"We are professionals," Glo clarified.

"Yes, that's it," Sabine agreed.

"I don't know about you," said Aja, "but I am a communicator."

"Just lay low with that idea, sweetie," said Glo. "You don't want to attract too much attention to it."

As Sabine and Glo left the switchboard room, they heard the handsome scanner voice dopple out with *"Psychiatric emergency, Charlie Level, Patient reporting either spiritual breakthrough or mental breakdown. Approach without lights or sirens. 2100."*

Chapter 7

Sabine had been shaped early on by Gene Roddenberry and the world on board the Starship Enterprise; Juliet by Bertolt Brecht's promise of a life with no rules, in The Rise and Fall of the City of Mahogany.

"Are we going straight to the rehab center or shall we stop for drinks first?" Glo said, turning down the sudden blast of Pandora's *Sex on the Beach Remix* station that accompanied Sabine's starting of the Volkswagen.

"What do you want to do?" Sabine backed out of her ER parking lot space and drove down the hill to Main Street.

"I wouldn't be thrilled about going sober to see Denize. Again. Hello."

"It's just that I have this strange feeling I need to get there quickly."

"It's six in the morning, how much quicker can anyone get anywhere, Sabine."

"Well now that we know it's six in the morning, where would we even go for drinks."

"Are you kidding me? This is Trummel."

"Okay then, Cumberland Farms. They have wine."

"No wait staff though. Why the rush to see Denize today?"

"It's just a feeling, I don't know. Something is up."

"I think you're reading too much into that nanosecond three weeks ago when you met Denize's eyes in the elevator and determined that the fate of the universe was contained in that transfer of information. You're sounding more and more like your crazy friend Juliet."

"Oh my God, Glo, you've fallen for it."

"For what?"

"Juliet is so abnormally pulled together that to the normal person she just appears crazy. The truth is, she's onto something."

Glo rolled her eyes. "Anyone who's pulled together is a mutant."

"She copes. What else is there?"

"Let's just get this over with."

"Do you have the stuff?"

"Yeah, the *Mission Impossible II* DVD and the CD of *Shirley Basse and the Propellerheads*. That was all I could find at the Walmart yesterday. And the quart of Carvel that I kept in the cafeteria freezer all day and didn't eat."

"Well, it's better to have shopped and not eaten than to have eaten and not shopped."

"Your logic is screwed up. 'Tis better to have shopped and not eaten than to not have shopped and ended up eating peanut butter on croutons because there's no food in the house."

"Huh. Better to have had the wine and thrown up than not to have had the wine and thrown up anyway."

"Better to have worried and have had it turn out to be nothing, than not to have worried and have had it be something. Are we there yet?"

Sabine parked in the Trummel Rehabilitation Center's icy front parking lot, pulled on the handbrake, and turned off the bug. The dry cold amplified the sounds of the women snapping off their seatbelts and getting out of the car. The wind was stiff and they squinted as they pulled their coats around them and walked into the lobby of the clean, one-story functional brick building.

"Where's the bar?" Glo said to the young nurses' aid at the front desk.

"Good morning, ladies." Naomi was wearing neon pink scrubs. A matching headband held back her sky blue hair, and her face, with no makeup, was fresh and uncomplicated.

"Hey Naomi, how's it going today?" Sabine said.

"It's going. Whatcha got?"

"*Mission Impossible II*, the *Propellerheads*, and a quart of Carvel," said Glo.

"Awesome. Hey, just walk on back to the gym. Denize is there with another visitor."

"She has friends?" said Sabine. Somehow it never occurred to her that Denize was anything other than a lost fawn. Speechless, she headed down the fluorescent-lit linoleum hall to the gym, with Glo behind her. And there was Denize in her wheelchair, in close conversation with Juliet Indigo, sitting on a bench press.

Juliet looked up at Sabine and Glo and smiled. Sabine froze. "Oh."

Glo, sensing an Incident, said "We have Carvel."

"Oh, excellent." Denize's voice was soft. "Wish I could eat it." The gym was tiny and dim, and Denize looked pale and gangly in her wheelchair, but at least she was dressed. She had traded in her rehab nightgown for jeans and a soft gray sweater. Her short brown hair, blunt cut with straight bangs, gave her a European look.

Glo brought her shopping bag of goodies over to Denize, and sat on the bench next to Juliet. She put the bag on the floor and shook off her floor-length padded nylon coat. Halfway through, Glo went into spurts of seizures to get the coat all the way off. A sleeve bopped Juliet's face as Glo put the coat in her lap. "Oops, sorry sweetie."

Juliet felt around her updo and fixed the strands of hair that had come undone. "That's okay."

Glo dug into her huge tote with both hands, emerging with three plastic spoons, a moist and drippy baggie with a pint of chocolate soft ice cream in it, and a toy airplane. "It's going to melt," she warned, tossing the plane back. "You can have my spoon, Juliet, I can't eat on an empty stomach anyway."

"I'm not hungry. You go at it."

"Here, Denize." She unzipped the sticky baggie and gave it to Denize. "Here's a spoon too. Sabine, come get your spoon."

"I'm not hungry either." Sabine joined the three and sat on a stack of mats on the other side of Denize. "You go ahead."

"I'm actually not that hungry," Denize ventured, checking out the three women to make sure this didn't offend anyone. She held the dripping carton out away from her. Glo took it back, sighed loudly, and got up from the bench. She took the melted Carvel to the cafeteria to throw it out, and Juliet whipped a compact out of thin air to check her hair.

"Denize was telling me about her grandmother," Juliet said to Sabine as she snapped her compact shut.

"I felt a connection, I'm not sure exactly why. That's why I came to visit."

All the times Sabine had visited Denize, she had never actually asked the girl anything personal. She didn't want to seem too eager for information, as if she were just being nice to Denize in order to find out about synchronicity and the meaning of life in Trummel. Then, too, as she got to know the teenager, she really liked her and didn't want to make her uncomfortable.

Denize had been out of high school for a year before the shooting happened. She had been living with an aunt and uncle in Trummel, and as far as Sabine could tell, there weren't any other relatives. "Naomi said she could dye my hair purple," Denize said. "What do you think?"

Juliet studied Denize's face as if she were evaluating a painting in a museum. Sabine consciously unraveled all the major muscle groups in her body as best she could. Why this newfound stress? Was she jealous that Juliet seemed so comfortable around people, while she had to work hard just to appear normal and unobtrusive? Was she jealous that Juliet had stolen Denize from her? Denize, her new pet project?

"Lavender, Denize. It's gentler," said Juliet.

"Lavender's good," Sabine echoed. "Or purple. Either one."

Denize turned in her wheelchair to look at Sabine. "You guys are so sweet to come and visit me all the time. I didn't know hospital people were this caring."

Naomi's pink scrubs grabbed everyone's attention as she wheeled in a handsome man in his forties and parked him across the gym by the parallel bars. They were followed by another man in a suit and tie, walking with a Bluetooth in his ear, speaking into an unseen cyberspace portal. "It was just his arm hairs that were burning, for Godsake. Get a grip."

"You ready to work?" Naomi said to her wheelchair man. "The physical therapist will be here in a minute."

"I'm ready for this to be over," he replied with an attempt at a smile. He was well-built, with gray around the temples, and a sparkle in his eye that looked like it was on the verge of going out.

The Bluetooth guy looked at him. "Listen, I gotta go. Hang tight. I'll be back later with the papers for you to sign, okay?"

The wheelchair man said "Yeah, but Dave I've got to get back to Cincinnati before they sign with someone else. It was a massive mistake coming here." He looked at Sabine, Juliet, and Denize. "Sorry, ladies, no offense. It's a very nice town, but I would have felt much better having had my stroke in Cincinnati."

Dave flashed the women a quick smile and then turned back to his friend. "I'll arrange for an ambulance to take you back home, Maz, don't worry. I'm working on it. It's a done deal."

"An ambulance to go from Trummel to Cincinnati?" Sabine said. "That's just not possible in the world as we know it."

Dave and Maz looked at Sabine.

"Oh. Sabine, this is Dave and this is Maz," said Naomi. "Sabine dispatches ambulances from the hospital for people we can't treat in Trummel."

Dave looked at his watch. He tapped Maz on the shoulder as if too busy to enter into a new conversation, and walked out of the gym saying to the portal, "I need the mileage from Trummel to Cincinnati." At the gym door he collided with Glo.

"I have no idea what that mileage would be," Glo answered, then did a double-take as her hunk radar kicked in. "Although I can find out for you, I'm sure."

But Dave was halfway down the hall.

"Or not." Glo joined the others by Denize.

"Maz, wait here," Naomi said as she sped out after Dave. "Did you bring that policy number I needed?" she said. "I can't think straight without a policy number." Her voice turned into a hall echo and then faded out.

The four women turned to look at Maz.

"What about helicopters?" he said to Sabine.

"Yeah, but not a medical helicopter," Sabine answered. "We need those for emergency traumas."

"I'm in a wheelchair. That's an emergency, right?"

"Not really."

"I'm a recovering alcoholic."

"So who isn't?"

"I had a stroke."

"You can't have a helicopter."

"I can't stay here, I'll die alone."

"You have Dave," Juliet offered. Her low voice and calm demeanor seemed to instantly relax him. The dwindling spark in his eyes flared a little before dimming back down. He wheeled himself across the small gym to the women.

"You have a beautiful voice," he said to Juliet.

"Oh - I'm not a dispatcher," Juliet said.

"I actually am a trained, um..." Glo began.

"Dispatcher," Sabine finished.

"Flight attendant," Glo corrected. "Continental Airlines. We got voice lessons."

"You're Juliet?" Maz was undeterred.

"I work at the switchboard, too," Sabine said, "but my specialty is trauma."

"Why yes," Juliet said to Maz.

"Your voice actually sounds familiar," he said.

"Really?"

"Yes. Have you been on television or in the movies?"

Sabine peeled herself off the stack of gym mats she was sitting on. "Denize, I got to go. Can I wheel you somewhere?" Glo stood up also.

"I guess to the front desk?" Denize said. "Naomi's going to do my hair lavender so I can join the ranks of the undead."

"You mean join the ranks of the living," Glo said as she took the handles on the back of the wheelchair, and pushed Denize toward the gym door. Sabine grabbed the coats and totes.

"Same thing, right?" Denize said. "Undead, living, undead, living?"

"Absolutely, sweetie," Sabine said.

As they pushed Denize over the gym threshold into the gray hallway, Sabine heard Juliet and Maz discussing the probability of a wormhole between Cincinnati and Budapest. Their voices faded into the deep background of overlaid echoes that fill the forgotten dimensions of old rooms.

Chapter 8

Sabine's amygdala overloaded upon visiting
Times Square on New Year's Eve in 1965. She
saw the giant news ticker, with its flashing
lights, announce fusion experiments in the
Mohave Desert that, if someone struck a match,
could ignite the earth's atmosphere. This was
important information.

Sabine always spent fifteen minutes of cat time
before leaving the condo for work. This was so she
could surround them with the white light of protection, a
little trick she learned in 1976 from the super in her
East Village apartment, Ariel, who was studying multi-
dimensional consciousness with Lama Govinda.

After surrounding the cats with white light,
Sabine would visualize her path to and from the
hospital, and see it cloaked in a golden glow of safety.

She often thought the gold was stronger than
the white, but was afraid to change her protocol for the
cats just in case she was wrong. The white had been
working. It would be too much of a gamble to mess with
it.

Also within her fifteen minute condo egress time,
she checked the stove and the iron, unplugged the
toaster, and turned on all the actual electric lights
except the one by the couch in the livingroom which

Freddie Mercury liked to knock over. She filled the condo with the blue light of peace so Dr. Crusher wouldn't throw up, and left a little catnip in Higgs-Boson's fort under the dining room table.

This was no mere psychological affliction. This was a carefully planned, non-reactive, non-hysterical, take-charge action protocol. The goal was to identify triggers before they happened, and then use that information to make sure they didn't happen. Like the *Star Trek* episodes where they go back in time to prevent some future apocalypse. Or like black ice in winter: You want to wear four-inch heels to work but you know you'll slip in the parking lot, so you don't wear the heels. It's proactively shifting events in time.

Her morning cat ritual completed, Sabine was relaxed and confident as she drove to the hospital. The sun was going down over Main Street and she refocused her emotional preparedness from cat protection to her job.

Running the switchboard and making overhead announcements were easy – she could do them in her sleep, and in fact often did. She had recurring dreams about trying to transfer calls to the emergency room using the corded Princess rotary dial phone from her teenage bedroom. It lit up. She loved it. Late at night, many years ago, as she lay awake, she knew her phone was right next to her and she felt connected. Safe.

Dispatching an ambulance to move a patient, though, in the present day, was stressful because there was no room for error. If the patient was intubated, you had to make sure the EMT team included a respiratory therapist. On the other hand, if the patient was merely going from hospital hip replacement surgery to rehab, you could breathe easy and tell the ambulance company that a Basic Level team was all they needed.

One time Sabine dispatched an ambulance for a lady who had swallowed her dentures and had to have emergency surgery. Trummel's ENT specialist had turned off his beeper and gone to Rhode Island where he was unreachable. The patient needed an Intermediate Level paramedic on board because she was still a choking risk. Sabine called Valley Ambulance, the last company on rotation, and had to talk them into taking the run. The Valley Ambulance EMTs thought swallowing dentures was boring. They lived for screaming through intersections as civilians pulled over on top of each other to clear the way. An EMT's neurological circuit was completed only with the electricity of near-death, the drama of a last gasp. Sabine got Valley Ambulance to take the denture lady only after promising them the very next pneumothorax.

The brain bleeds and the stemis that came into Trummel Hospital's emergency room were the most nerve-racking because they were emergent. Sabine's job was to get the ambulance to the patient within a ten minute time frame, so they could be whisked away to another hospital before anything horrible happened. "We need you here, lights and sirens."

Trummel only had three ambulance companies. The Fire Department 911 ambulance was reserved mainly for car wrecks - so when the three private ambulances in the town were all en route to somewhere and a head trauma would come in, Sabine had to triage - call the less urgent ambulances back for the head traumas, and re-schedule the gangrenous toes for later in the night when things settled down.

If it was a full moon and everyone was having head traumas and their trach tubes were falling out, Dispatch often ran out of ambulances. That means if you're having a heart attack on a snowy Saturday night when everyone else is fracturing their hips at the ski slope, you're going to need to learn how to pray.

But nothing took precedence over a stemi, the most dangerous stage of a heart attack. Trummel Hospital didn't have cardiac specialists who could handle stemis, although they were looking for one. The actual cardiac rock stars practiced at the big venues in

Manhattan. So when a stemi came into the Trummel ER, Lulu always called Sabine to dispatch an ambulance to Trummel Hospital, stat, to rush the patient to New York before they coded.

Her mental rehearsals and reviews completed for that evening, Sabine drove her VW into the ER parking lot in the back of the building. She quickly completed the planning of her day by imagining herself back at home at dawn after a smooth and well-run shift, sipping a glass of Firehouse Merlot, safe and cozy, happily cleaning up cat vomit. Cat vomit was easy. She wished more of life was cat vomit.

An overnight nurse pulled in to the parking space next to her, with a muffled Al Jarreau singing "All I need is to get my boogie down" from inside her car.

Sabine was exhausted from pre-identifying the night's panic triggers, but knew that immersion into the night's crises in the dimly lit Telecommunications cave - focusing completely on saving insulin overdoses and assault victims - would resuscitate her.

Glo was already there, plugged in and immersed. She and Sabine exchanged silent hellos and Sabine hung her coat on the back of the door and unloaded Fig Newtons and cranberry juice from her tote. Glo was telling her caller, "If you're peeing blood, then the answer is yes, you should come to the emergency room." She clicked a button and took one ear off her headset. "Good evening, Mademoiselle."

"Hey," answered Sabine. "How's it going?"

"I just got on. Valentine said the day shift phones were super busy and they ran out of ambulances. Now we have at least one ambulance company back and ready."

"I hope we don't get two sick people."

"I'm glad I don't run this place, I only work here."

"I'm glad they don't know we're here in the cave making things happen. You want to keep things running smoothly you have to lay low."

Over the police scanner, the handsome disembodied male voice said *"Person hanging in tree, Milltown Cemetery, Signal 21."*

Signal 21 was an attempted suicide. A really bad idea because who's to say that on the other side you don't have the exact same issues you had on this side, with the difference being that now you don't have a body so you can't fix it.

Oddly, though, Trummel Hospital had an ever increasing number of people coming in after attempted suicides. Life was a landmine, Sabine got that. She settled into her computer station. "Thank you for calling Trummel Hospital, this is Sabine, how can I help you?"

"Yes, can you put me through to the, uh…
what's the name of that place?"

"The Emergency Room?"

"No, the place where you go when you get run
over."

"The ER?"

"Yes, that's the one."

"Hold while I transfer you."

"Speaking of which, Sabine," Glo said, taking
her headset off and standing up. "Henry Moho came by
again."

"Uh oh."

Glo locked her hands over her head and
stretched up as high as she could, standing on her
tiptoes. Some sort of knee pain kicked in and she fell
back into her chair. "Yeah. He said there's a meeting
you're supposed to go to tonight. 7:00 in the
conference room."

"Me?"

"Yeah. He's taken a shine to you, don't you
think?"

"He didn't even know we still had a Telecomm
department."

"It's all very scary, Sabine. Were you able to
decipher those files he gave you?"

"No. Maybe that's what the meeting is about."

"Bring the files with you, just in case. Maybe he's got a cryptographer for them."

"Okay."

On her way up to the conference room on the second floor to meet Henry Moho, Sabine heard Glo over the loudspeaker. *"Sabine Covina please call extension 0720. Extension 0720. Thank you, Sabine Covina."* Sabine stopped at the wall phone near Telemetry, the cardiac unit, and entered Henry's extension, 0720. She was startled when it actually connected to somewhere and Henry picked up.

"The Psych Unit admin - yeah, I know, the PUF people - have taken the conference room," Henry said. *"I could kick them out, I mean I have that authority, but they're thinking of changing their name to Behavioral Health."*

"Okay," Sabine said.

"But the chapel is empty," Henry said. *"Why don't you meet me in the chapel instead."*

"Okay."

Room 245, the hospital chapel, was at the end of the floor in Telemetry. It was a small room, but Facilities had installed stained glass windows, and a podium with a Bible. Two flickering flameless candles looked out on four rows of pews. Next to the podium in a large floor flowerpot was a huge arrangement of dusty silk flowers.

The room was empty when Sabine got there, so she sat in the front pew, facing the podium. She felt like she was intruding. People came here in crisis, when their loved ones were in surgery or didn't make it. She didn't want to be hogging this space if someone needed it.

Henry came in before she could give it more thought, carrying more paper files. "Did the files I gave you the other day help with your situation?"

Sabine had learned at the beginning of her corporate hospital career how to carry on entire conversations without knowing what was being discussed. "I'm still sorting through them, Henry, thanks. So, what's up?"

Henry paced back and forth in front of the podium. "We were supposed to be automating the Telecommunications Department."

"Yes."

"Well it's still not automated."

"Oh. Yes. What's up with that."

"We got the lab an AA with a tree. And HR and Public Relations have them too. The AAs free up personnel."

Sabine always associated AA with Bill W., the original GoToMeeting guy, but in AdminSpeak it stood for Automated Answering. The "tree" was the number of choices the caller had to sit through before pushing the next button, which in the case of the lab, triggered a second AA and another series of options.

"I know. Henry, are you aware that the doctors hate the lab's AA? Everyone hates it. They complain to us operators that they can never get to a person. They call me and instead of asking me to connect them to the lab, they state unequivocally that they want to speak to a live person in the lab. Any person, any part of the lab."

"The doctors don't see the big picture, Sabine."

"Mass General called the other day needing an emergency bloodwork update on a patient we sent them with jumping lumberjack syndrome. Mass General couldn't get past our lab's phone tree. The guy was seizing while Mass General listened to the voice prompts. I had to overhead page the lab to tell them to answer their phone."

Henry studied Sabine as she spoke, which Sabine interpreted as interest.

She continued. "Dr. Raj said the lab's AA was evil. That was the word he used, Henry. Evil."

"Dr. Raj?" Henry said.

"Our ER doctor."

"Yes." Henry sat down at the end of Sabine's pew. Sabine imagined they were spies sitting at a park bench trying to exchange intel with one speaking Mandarin and the other speaking Portuguese.

"And Lulu had someone hemorrhaging the other day," Sabine continued, "and needed the lab to do some tests on him stat. She was in a hurry so she clicked on the lab's extension and got seven minutes' worth of automated options. She called me at the switchboard and I was able to get her through on a back line."

"Did he expire?"

"No, Lulu brought him back to life."

"That's wonderful. Who's Lulu?"

"What is our meeting about, Henry?"

Henry shuffled through the manila files on his lap. Sabine saw his badge dangling from his lariat, but it was still backwards and mostly hidden by his tie, so there was still no clue about what department he was from.

She thought she'd try an experiment. "By the way, Henry, I heard you got promoted to, um…in the um, department of…"

Henry looked up and held out his stack of files to Sabine. "Oh, yes, thank you."

Sabine took the files. She'd have Nyx check into this. Surely Nyx could find out if someone got promoted somewhere.

"So I take it Telecomm still is using operators."

"Yes, Henry. We absolutely can't have a phone tree. When people call the hospital they need to speak to a warm, caring voice that can decipher what they're trying to say."

"Alright, dear, I tell you what. I'll put the Telecomm AA project on hold for now, mainly because I need you to finish up with these files. But the review committee will meet again next month to see what they want to do."

One of the flameless candles went out.

"Don't forget what happened to Dr. Fu the day we had that Code Gray last month in the ICU, Henry. Remember? I wrote up a report. Dr. Fu pressed that panic button you have installed there, but the panic button was never connected to anywhere. Dr. Fu called Aja over the regular phone lines and Aja put her on hold because the switchboard was overflowing. By the time Aja filtered through the phone line rotation and got to Dr. Fu's call, Dr. Fu was on the floor with the woman's hands around her throat.

"Oh yes, the Code Gray."

"The patient coded and his wife tried to strangle Dr. Fu, remember?"

"Who's Aja?"

"She's an operator, Henry. She got security up there in one minute. You need humans at the switchboard."

"My dear Sabine, is that a threat? There's an Incident file on you, you know."

Sabine straightened her new stack of files and stood up. "I know."

Henry stood up too. "You know?"

"Of course."

"Well okay, then, see what you can do with these files, will you dear? They're important."

"So, what department are the files from, anyway." She walked toward the door, hoping to get some Intel without appearing like she didn't know anything.

"Very funny, Sabine. Now watch yourself. And thank you."

"You're welcome."

As Sabine left the chapel she brushed by a young couple coming in. The man was pale as a marshmallow and the woman had two streaks of black mascara trailing down each cheek.

"...and I was crawling across this shaky suspension bridge. Crawling," the woman was whispering.

"What happened?" the man asked.

"I don't know. I woke up."

One of the things Sabine noticed about Juliet was that she kept her condo at eighty-five degrees. "It's these winters," Juliet said as she tucked one leg under her on the sectional and grabbed a beige cashmere throw for her lap.

"We need to get you some cats, Jule," Sabine said. "My cats keep me warm at night."

"You sleep with cats?" Juliet said this as if she were saying "You sleep on the ceiling?".

There was an opened bottle of Firehouse Station Red Engine Company 5 Merlot and two Tiffany wine glasses on the low livingroom coffeetable. Sabine had her stack of manila file folders in her arms which she plopped down next to the wine as she sat across from Juliet on a soft loveseat. Juliet carefully poured a little into each glass, slowly and with great concentration, like a tea ceremony.

The Merlot ritual always had a calming effect for Sabine. The visual of wine still in the bottle was reassuring. You didn't necessarily have to drink the wine to feel the buzz - it was enough to just know it was there. To see it looking lovely and delicate in a pretty glass and to know there was more in the bottle - and more bottles in the cabinet - made Sabine feel like she was in the midst of a thick golden cloud. Knowledge was everything.

"Oh yes, I've always slept with bunches of cats. Even when there were husbands in the mix. Cats are such good sleepers, it's inspiring."

Juliet laughed. "I'll just borrow yours, Sabine. I'm more of a cat grandmother in that I like to give the babies back at the end of the day."

"What about your husband?" Ah ha! Sabine realized this was the exact perfect time to ask. "Surely he can keep you warm."

"He's around somewhere." Juliet leaned forward and slowly wrapped her long red nails around the bottom of her glass.

"Around somewhere here in your condo?"

"Sometimes. He's not well, you know. Oh my God, we need some music. Then you can tell me what you're doing with all those files." Juliet put the throw around her shoulders and padded barefoot through the deep beige carpet to her media center in the corner. She was wearing a pair of loose black silk slacks and an oversized beigy-pink sweater. Her hair was caught up in a high ponytail with soft strands falling out. As she fiddled with controls at the media center, the recessed lights from the ceiling caught her diamond stud earrings and made them sparkle. It was only four in the afternoon, but for Sabine it was Happy Hour since she had to be at work again at eleven.

"What's wrong with your husband?" Sabine said. She knew she was pushing it, and that Juliet was trying to change the subject, but this was information and they were living in the Information Age.

"Tristan."

Sabine nearly fell over. Today was a good day for Intel. Maybe she'd have the same luck deciphering Henry's files. "Tristan."

Juliet sighed as she clicked things on her media computer, careful out of habit to use the pads of her fingers so as not to break any nails. She turned toward Sabine. "Yes. He's been in and out of remission with this awful lymphoma. He's a physicist. He does night vision stuff."

"Oh my God, Juliet, I didn't know."

"I like to keep the house warm. He's away on a lecture tour right now, but he gets cold very easily."

"Is he in remission right now?"

"He just disappears sometimes."

At this discontinuity jump, Sabine knew it was time to back off. Juliet had her own personal coping devices, whatever they might be, and they seemed to be working. "Well then, put on some music for concentration," Sabine said. "I need you to help me de-encrypt this stuff that admin gave me."

Juliet turned back to her entertainment center. "Who's admin?" The music clicked on: *Where Were You (Sunday Afternoon)* by Evolve, from **Happy Hour in the Gene Pool**. Soft, pulsing electronica muffled in front of a velvet string wash. Perfect soundtrack music for figuring out life. She swayed gently to the music as she came back to the conversation area.

"I don't know exactly who admin is," Sabine answered. "This guy, Henry Moho, but for all I know he's an alien from outer space and no one can see him except me."

"In that case, let's see the files and don't worry about a thing."

"I'm probably not supposed to have brought them out of the hospital."

"All the better." Juliet sat down on the couch and picked up her wine glass. "I will be your file whisperer."

Sabine spread the files out casino style, like cards. Both women looked in silence at the file names: Aside from the acronym LIBAD, nothing was decipherable. Juliet opened the top file labeled Q, and took out pages filled with columns of numbers, all written in by hand.

"First we have to establish why he's using paper files and an actual pen in the first place. That's as much of a puzzle as what's in them," said Juliet.

"The medium is the message," Sabine said, remembering the Marshall McLuhan craze in 1967. She remembered it because that was the year she saw Monica Vitti and Terence Stamp in *Modesty Blaise* and realized that she wanted to do something fabulous with her life. She had taken singing lessons, and although she was able to develop a warm, rich tone, her vocal range consisted of just the one note. She took an acting class with less than encouraging results and finally settled for smoking Nat Sherman Fantasia Cigarettes, coordinating the cigarette colors with her outfits. After a week of that she gave it up and found that she was able to get work doing medical voiceovers.

The voiceover work was Sabine's entry into the healthcare industry. She narrated videos demonstrating everything from an aortic aneurysm repair to spinal fusion surgery. She established herself, in a small way, as an expert in narrating medical procedures without tripping over words, and she had a knack for describing all kinds of terrifying conditions without emotion. That was the key, to remain the observer and not get lost in the horror of it all.

"His information is on paper, not in cyberspace," said Juliet. "That by itself is telling us something."

Sabine looked at the files. She moved from the loveseat to the floor to get closer, and shuffled through them, opening them at random to see if anything made any more sense. "Okay," she said, summing up their findings. "So we know. These are paper files."

Juliet put her drink down and picked up a pair of drug store reading glasses. She rearranged some of the files. "I'm sensing a pattern here."

"You see something?"

"Yes."

"What?"

Juliet carefully picked out papers from the top file that was labeled BO, and placed them thoughtfully next to some other papers that had fallen out, as if she were arranging a hand of cards.

"Look at this." She had four pages. Each one had a bold letter in the upper left corner in an oriental looking font.

"It spells BOAT."

There was a hushed moment of awe. No one spoke, no one drank. Then Sabine took a deep breath. "Okay, Juliet." She smiled and picked up her wine glass. "Something about a boat."

At the hospital later, between answering calls, overhead announcing Rapid Response Teams to help people who were passing out or having seizures, and dispatching ambulances to rush ER patients to Manhattan for pacemakers, Sabine fantasized about the handsome disembodied male voice coming through the police scanner. *"Stunned person, 15 Elm Street, Bravo level. Stunned person, 15 Elm Street, Bravo level. 1936."* If I were standing in the middle of Elm Street, stunned, Sabine thought, whoever is attached to that voice would be the man I would want to come save me.

Chapter 9

Sabine's life was shaped early on by Jean-Paul Sartre's Nausea and also by Sit Down You're Rockin' the Boat from Guys and Dolls, both studies in dream-states. Juliet's early years were sprinkled with blackouts and lost time brought on by being immersed in Proust's À la recherche du temps perdu.

Sabine ran down the hall to Telecomm, although in high heeled boots it was not all that fast. The phones were ringing like sirens, and Glo's workstation was empty. At Glo's station was steaming coffee in a chipped mug with "Wifey" written on it – possibly half of a once-pair of mugs from Glo's distant past, the mate of which might have said "Hubby" - an uncapped pen, and reminder notes containing doctors' pager numbers and a partially filled-out Code Blue checklist.

"Thank you for calling Trummel Hospital, this is Sabine, can you hold please? Thank you. Thank you for calling Trummel Hospital, can you hold? Thank you. Thank you for calling Trauma Town, hold please, thank you." Then back to the top. "Thank you for holding, how can I help you?"

"We've changed our minds. Tell them to resuscitate him!" a woman's voice shrieked. Then the

line went dead. Sabine had the computer redial the number, but after one ring it went to a voicemail that was full.

Sabine froze while she searched her mind for some way to act on this. The blinking lights from the other calls would have to wait. She glanced at the Code Blue form on Glo's desk. It indicated an acute disseminated encephalomyelitis– a brain and spinal column emergency – you can't live without your brain and spinal column – from four minutes ago. The nurse must have called next of kin, the wife, and the hysterical caller could have been her.

Sabine called up to the nurses' station on Three. No one answered. Sabine tried calling Room 336 directly - with a code in progress, that's probably where everyone was. Still no answer. She grabbed her radio.

"Switchboard to Security, come in please."

No response.

"Switchboard to Security, urgent, come in please."

What seemed like years passed. *"This is Security. I can't talk right now."*

"Security, yes talk. Call me at the switchboard at extension zero, stat."

Four of her lines were still blinking, and the fifth line rang. Sabine recognized the phone number as the hysterical woman, and she grabbed it. "This is the hospital."

"Did you tell them? We changed our mind, we want him resuscitated!"

"Mrs. Boulevard?"

"Yes, yes. I'm on my way." She hung up again. Sabine redialed her number, but again it went to a functionless voicemail.

Line five rang again, this time from Room 336. "Switchboard, Sabine speaking."

"Yeah, it's Eusebio from Security."

"Mrs. Boulevard called. She said they've changed their minds and she wants her husband resuscitated."

"Stand by." Some shuffling, then another voice -

"Sabine, this is Sunami, the nurse on Three. We're trying to keep him alive until the family decides what's going on. Are they coming in?"

"Yes, they're on their way."

"What's their ETA?"

"Her phone had a Danville-on-Hudson exchange," Sabine said. "So she could be half an hour away with no traffic."

"We'll do everything we can, but half an hour is going to be a long time. He's hanging on by a thread, and I mean that."

Incoming calls overflowed to Glo's empty workstation. Where was she?

"Understood." Sabine clicked the extension for the first waiting caller. "Thank you for -"

"*Sabine, it's Glo.*"

"Glo?"

"*Yeah.*"

"Your, uh, coffee is here at your desk."

"*I know. I had to throw up.*"

"Hang on." Sabine put Glo on hold and worked her way through the blinking switchboard. "Thank you for holding, how can I direct your call?"

"*I'm calling from Florida.*"

"Who would you like to speak to?"

"*I'm not sure, maybe you could help me. This all began in 1983 when I had hip replacement surgery there at your hospital --- wait, or was it 1984?*"

"M'am, can you hold again please?" She punched in line 2. "Thank you for holding, how can I help you?"

"*What time is the AA meeting tonight?*"

"Hold, please, I'll get their hotline number for you." Line 3. "Thank you for holding, how can I help you?"

"*My thumb is getting bigger and bigger.*"

"Okay, I'm putting you through to the ER." Line 4: "Thank you for ---"

"There are no drug stores open."

"Ooo, yes, nothing's open past six here in Trauma Town."

"What?"

"I mean Trummel. Here in Trummel. If it's an emergency there are twenty-four hour pharmacies in the City." Click to next caller. "How can I –"

"I so totally can't do this anymore." The caller's voice sounded like cigarettes and breathless horror. *"it's gone beyond what I can do. Don't call anybody, I mean I'm not going to commit suicide or anything."*

"Can you hold on long enough for me to put you through to someone?"

"It doesn't matter..."

"Is there someone there who could bring you into our Emergency Room?"

"No."

The protocol for suicide calls had never really been set. You just had to get them to not hang up while you transferred their call to the ER, and then pray that someone in the ER would actually pick up.

One time a man called and said he was in the process of cutting himself with a razor and there was blood everywhere. Fortunately Barbara Vermouth from PR was in the switchboard room trying to talk Glo and

Sabine into stuffing donation envelopes for the upcoming hospital gala, and Barbara was tight with Naruma Dimitri the per diem spiritual advisor who happened to be at work that day. Sabine was able to talk to the guy until Barbara could confirm that Naruma was at her phone and would actually answer. Sabine told the man, "There's this really really nice person who wants to talk to you, okay?" And he said okay and the call was transferred. No one knew how it turned out, because Naruma joined Doctors Without Borders and was gone the next day, leaving Trauma Town with yet another spiritual advisory gap.

Sabine transferred the new suicide call to the ER. It was safer than trying to get him to write down an 800 suicide prevention number where you had to press 3 to speak to someone.

The dim light from the hall fluttered as Glo rushed in. "So so so sorry, sweetie," she said, sliding into her chair, grabbing her headset, and spilling the coffee at her workstation. "Shit." She got up and ran out.

"Glo, forget it," Sabine said, "I need you. The sick people of Trummel need you. I'll page Nyx to come clean up the spill, my earlobe is falling off."

Glo stopped as if she had run into an invisible wall, then slowly turned back to face Sabine. "Deep breath," she said in her overhead announcement voice. She moved slowly to her workstation and reattached herself to the computer. She clicked on one of the blinking lights, mopping up some of the coffee with a scratchy brown paper towel she had brought in from the bathroom. "This is Operator Glo, thank you for calling Trummel Hospital, how may I be of great help to you?" She sounded stoned, but Sabine knew Glo was straight as an arrow. At least now at this point in her later life.

Back in the day, when it was the rage, Glo had been on all sorts of doctor prescribed things, especially Valium. Now that no one was taking that stuff anymore, Glo had described how, instead of prayer or meditation every day which her therapist swore by, she tried to reverse engineer the feeling of having taken a Valium.

She had developed this reverse-engineering technique after her near-brush with the Trummel postal inspector when she ordered vitamins from an online supplier in Yucatan after her breakup with the fireman. Glo had known they weren't exactly vitamins, but still she couldn't sleep and was willing to give whatever they were a try. Fortunately, the postal inspector got bored with her fairly quickly because no one could sleep ever, even the postal inspector, so he moved on to more prolific and dependable vitamin dealers, many from the far more glamorous New Jersey.

The technique was to generate opiates naturally, through the power of intention. Sabine had come in one day excited about having read Shakti Gawain's *Creative Visualization*, and Glo was in crisis, so she figured what the heck.

The beauty of generating opiates through the power of intention, was that it was completely legal, had no side effects, and you could take a jillion of these mental Valiums a hundred times a day. A dream come true. "I'm set for life," Glo had said with the prayerful relief of one who had won the lottery. It was perfect, except that it didn't work.

Sabine paged Nyx to come to Telecomm to clean up Glo's coffee spill. Not a bad enough spill to call a Code Orange, but still, they needed information and Nyx was the one to call. And even when a spill was bad – like when the corpse exploded in the morgue last year, which would be a quintessential Code Orange, especially since the body was filled with antibiotic-resistant superbugs – managers hesitated to call Code Oranges because it was bad press for their departments.

The pungent fragrance of Avon *Exotic Nights* filled the switchboard room.

"Nyx!" Glo said. "Thank freaking God."

Nyx paused in the doorway, the fluorescent light from the hall framing the blond bedhead wisps that escaped from her French twist. "Hello, ladies." This was the voice of power that came from knowing things.

"Thanks for answering our page," said Sabine.

"I go where I'm needed." Nyx came a few steps into the room and stood with her weight evenly on both feet, Kill-Bill style. She was wearing lavender scrubs decorated with pictures of cats' facial expressions, and holding a red biohazard bag. She looked at the bag as if its presence surprised her, then exchanged it in her housekeeping cart with a rag. "You paged me about the guy in 336, I assume?" she said as she mopped up the coffee at Glo's workstation.

"Did Mrs. Boulevard make it here in time to say goodbye?"

"She did, Sabine. The police escorted her in with a great deal of fuss, and Nurse Sunami was out front to meet her and drag her upstairs. Justin Boulevard passed away a few minutes after. A happy ending, no?"

"I guess," Sabine said.

"As happy as cardiomyopathy," Glo said, and clicked on a blinking light. "Hippity hoppity, how may I direct your call?"

Sabine, Nyx, and Glo then paused in mid-movement, not wanting to miss a syllable, as the handsome disembodied scanner voice interrupted with, *"Staggering person, Black Cat Café, Alpha Level. Staggering person, Black Cat, 0200."*

"Gotta go," Nyx said, turning around, grabbing her housekeeping cart in the hall, and disappearing.

Sabine turned to her computer and clicked on a blinking light. "Thank you for calling ---"

"Yes, I found this number on my caller ID."

"You've reached the hospital switchboard. Was there a voicemail or an extension number on your caller ID so I can better direct your call?"

"It's my daughter with the two kittens. She took the kittens in."

"Is your daughter a patient here?"

"No, she took the car."

Sabine clicked on her MedTrakker icon to pull up the list of inpatients. "What's your daughter's name?" Her hands were poised over her keyboard, ready to input a name.

"She took the kittens in to the doctor."

"Oh, okay, this is not an animal hospital."

"An animal hospital, yes, thank you. My daughter took the kittens in."

"M'am, actually we're a people hospital."

"What?"

"A place where sick people come."

"Well then where are the kittens?" She was indignant.

"Your daughter might have taken them to the vet."

"This isn't the vet?"

"No, I'm really sorry."

"Well why did you call me?" She hung up.

Sabine's cell phone vibrated on the desk. She looked down at a new text message. It was from Glo. *HENRY MOHO. INCOMING.*

"Glo, I'm right here, you don't have to text ---"

Henry Moho was actually standing in the switchboard room. Sabine did not hear him approaching. It was as if he beamed in there silently from wherever his molecules hung out. Sabine took off her headset and swirled her chair around. "Yes Henry. What can we at Telecomm do for you?"

Henry was looking around with wonder and suspicion as if he had just materialized on an alien planet by mistake. "You're still here."

"Yes. Yes we are." Indecipherable reconn, handled deftly, she thought.

"Have you finished with those files yet?"

"Oh – are they time sensitive? You didn't –"

"Yes, Sabine. In fact, let's make them a top priority."

"What about –"

"The files. Top priority."

"What about the patients?"

"No, the files. The files." He disappeared into the hall and faded into nothingness.

"He could be the anti-Christ," Glo said to Sabine as she clicked off her next call. "We just don't know."

"They sent you home from x-ray without your clothes?" Sabine said to line 4. "Can you hold, please, sir, while I transfer you to our Embedded Guest Coordinator Issue Resolution Specialist?" Then to Glo. "Juliet's helping me decipher the files. She thinks there might be something there."

"Of course there's something there. Prehistoric cave drawings."

"No, it's something about, um, a boat. We got that far. And Juliet has been talking to Denize, who actually apparently knows Clea."

"Denize the shootee and Clea the shooter?"

"Yeah."

"The Clea who's now in the Program Unit Facility?"

"Yes, in the psych unit. They both have grandmothers, and there's a document somewhere."

"Wow, good work," Glo said, and clicked on line 3. "Thank you for calling Trummel Hospital … pseudogout starts with a 'p'. I have no idea, Sir, I just know that all that stuff starts with a 'p'. Fine, start it with an 's'." She clicked on line 4.

Because Sabine and Juliet liked to keep up with the arts, and with not a wide range of cultural activities occurring in Trummel, they sometimes had to go down the street to the Park View Nursing Home to hear the various piano recitals, poetry slams, and debates about the environment. This evening's offering was a lecture highlighting Deep Vein Thrombosis Awareness Month, followed by a Yoga for Arthritis demonstration.

The dining room, where the events took place, was huge and airy, and done in whites, yellows, and light beiges, which made Sabine happy because she felt she could twirl around in the hallways and not hit anything, although her left hip had been bothering her lately.

Juliet liked Park View Nursing Home because there were mirrors everywhere so she could check her makeup, and the decor had a baroque feel with curly details, which reminded her of Copenhagen. She had never been to Copenhagen, but in 1976 she had read Julian Jaynes' *The Origin of Consciousness in the Breakdown of the Bicameral Mind*, and she realized that experience was non-local.

Sabine and Juliet sat in the back because they knew, experientially, that a sudden attack of extreme acute boredom was highly possible, in which case they'd need immediate egress.

"We really should get into the City," Juliet said. "It's not that long a drive."

"Six hours," Sabine said.

"I can make it in seven."

"You're right, for sure. We need to do that."

They slid their winter coats off onto the folding chair backs. The round tables were set for the next meal, with large china plates, cloth napkins, heavy silverware, and stemmed water glasses.

In the front of the dining room the speaker tapped his microphone. "Welcome to Park View Nursing Home's lecture and arts series." He cleared his throat. "Before we start I just want to remind everyone that next month is Antiphospholipid Syndrome Awareness week."

Sabine leaned toward Juliet. "I love that we get out and do things."

"Even when there's nothing to do," Juliet agreed.

"We're proactive."

"And that's a good thing. Eckhart Tolle says you bring your stuff to where you are, rather than you move to a place and let the place do stuff to you."

"Ooo, that's good," Sabine said.

"So it's like, we're here, dressed up and looking great, at a lecture. It doesn't matter that we're not in Copenhagen."

"So true!"

Sabine and Juliet turned to face the front of the dining room, where the speaker was beginning. "Two senior citizens walk into a bar," he said.

Juliet leaned toward Sabine. "Ready?"

"Yep."

The women discreetly picked up their coats, slipped out of the dining room into the hall, and headed for the door.

And there was Raphael, the reporter for the *Trummel Sun*, hogging the entire doorway.

"Oops," said Sabine.

Raphael unzipped his black Northface Men's Thermoball. One glove was in his mouth and the other on the floor. "Hey," he said, and the glove fell out of his mouth.

"Hey," Sabine said. "You're here for the lecture?"

"Oh, it's not a wine tasting? We listed wine tasting in the paper for tonight." Raphael picked up his gloves.

"You'll like this better," Sabine said.

"By the way," Raphael said. "You guys heard the latest about your little hospital shooter, right?"

"She's been in the Program Unit Facility," Sabine said. "That's all I know. Our informant still hasn't been credentialed to go in there and clean. Why, what's up?"

Raphael smiled. Juliet smiled back.

"You guys leaving?" Raphael asked.

"Oh for God's sake. What's up with Clea in the Psych Unit?" Sabine said.

"What's up is that they let her out."

Sabine pulled her gloves from her coat pocket. "Loose?"

"She was so little," Juliet said.

Raphael laughed. "She charmed the doctor, and the police don't have enough evidence to hold her."

"Maybe she didn't do it," Juliet said.

Sabine was surprised to feel a bolt of indignation. "How did you get this information?" She was more upset about him having information that she didn't have, than she was at the fact that Clea was running around Trauma Town with a possible gun.

"I have connections. I'm a high profile reporter. I used to live in New York."

Juliet turned to Sabine. "He used to live in New York."

"The East Village," Raphael said.

And then Sabine realized. Raphael was a portal to the wide, outer universe of unlimited information gathering. It was who he was. He had connections that were better than Sabine's. He needed to be befriended. He had been in the East Village when Blondie was performing at CBGB's. He had access.

Both women looked at Raphael as if sizing him up for an assignment.

Raphael's confident smile faded. "What?"

A young couple, possibly a daughter and son-in-law of one of the nursing home residents, walked in the front door past Raphael.

"It's the end of the world," said the daughter.

"You say that like it's a bad thing," said the son-in-law.

Chapter 10

Sabine was shaped early on by the Ave Maria scene at the end of Disney's Fantasia. Raphael was informed in his early years by Patti LaBelle's Lady Marmalade.

"*Gitcha gitcha ya ya, da da,*" was coming through the speakers.

"Fix that right now, Raphael, on pains of death." Sabine was sitting on the floor in Juliet's livingroom, draped over Henry's files on the glass coffee table.

Raphael was walking in circles, muttering something about the East Village being better than the West Village. He stopped in front of Juliet's entertainment corner. "Okay," he said. "So let's see. She has a station called *Eurochill*, and one called *Cosmic Debris* by *Radio Free Brooklyn*."

"*Cosmic Debris*. Then come look at these files. I may have outsmarted the code."

Raphael clicked some keys on the entertainment console and a light-velvet, string-washed sound-breeze suitable for someone's life's background music, floated through the room. He turned to Sabine. "Where's our hostess?"

"Oh. She went for a walk. We exchanged keys. She feeds my cats when I work double shifts, and I come to her place when I need to decrypt codes."

"Got it." Raphael sat on the floor opposite Sabine. "And, uh, her, you know."

"Husband?"

"Yeah, that."

"Oh." Sabine looked up from the manila files that were scattered over the table. "That would be Tristan." She felt a deep thrill knowing something Raphael didn't.

"Yeah. I never see her with him. Are they ... together?"

"Raphael, for Godsake. Besides you're much too young for her. She and Tristan go way back."

"Yeah. So is he...what does he do? I mean..."

"They adore each other."

"So you've met him?"

"No."

"What's his thing?"

"I don't know. He travels a lot. He's been sick."

Raphael got up from the couch and walked around again, his heavy ski socks sinking silently into the deep carpet. The boots had come off at the door. Even if it wasn't one of Juliet's requirements, there was no way anyone could enter her condo with shoes on, let alone LLBean Knife Edge waterproof suede hiking boots. Crystal vases and prismatic decanters sat on dark floating bookshelves. "I don't see any, like, family photos anywhere."

"Oh well, you know, who knows."

"Have you ever seen a picture of him? Does she at least carry a photo on her phone?"

"Focus, Raphael. We have a job to do here. You said you'd help me break this code in exchange for an exclusive. All we know is that these files have something to do with, um, apparently, a boat. We need to dig deeper, *boat* doesn't tell me anything about my department being replaced by automated answering software."

The front door rattled and Juliet came in, dressed in a beige running suit with a gold silk scarf. "I'm back," she said, holding the wall with one hand while she pulled off her sneakers. Her cheeks were red from the cold. She peeled off her gloves and placed them on the spotless, dustless dark wood console table by the front door.

"Hey. How was your walk?" Raphael said.

"It made me thirsty. I saw a dead goose." She disappeared into the kitchen. "Did you finish deciphering those crazy files?" she called.

"Someone's having trouble focusing," Sabine called back.

Juliet came back into the room and then slipped down another hall into her bedroom. "Did you guys get the wine I left out for you?" she called.

"Not yet," Sabine called back. "We were waiting for you."

"So where's, uh, Tristan?" Raphael called down the hall.

"It's really weird," Juliet called back. "Deepak says we are all one, right? Like we're all fragments of the same ... hmm. Of the same ..."

"Vibrating energy field," Raphael yelled back.

"That's it! You're cute, Raphael. Don't you think, Sabine?"

"Oh yes. But you left me back at vibrating energy field."

Juliet appeared in the livingroom wearing an icy silver chiffon sweat pant set with rhinestones in the hoodie. Her head was tilted as she stuck a diamond earring into her ear. "So when I'm on my walks, I look and I don't see anybody. I mean my soul floats along above me as I walk through the neighborhoods but it never meets anyone up there. Deepak, Eckhart, Wayne, Neil deGrasse, everyone – says we're all, like 'one'. But when I float around in my spirit self, I don't see anyone else. If we're all one, how come I feel so alone? Where is everybody?"

Sabine chose not to speak in lieu of saying something stupid, and she figured Raphael was silent because he was trying to work up something meaningful and it wasn't coming.

Juliet took the wine bottle and three glasses from the kitchen bar and brought them over to the coffeetable. Plunging the wine opener into the top of the bottle, she said, "I just don't want my faith to be shaken."

"What faith is that?" Raphael asked.

"My stuff. I've carefully put together a belief system over the years that lets me survive in this godforsaken wasteland of a dimension. I have to believe my stuff, even though it may not be true. You know of course this is the hell dimension, right?"

"I've known that for quite some time," Raphael said.

Juliet pulled the cork out of the Merlot.

Sabine listened to and felt deep gratitude for the cork's soft popping sound followed by the whimsical gurgling of the wine being poured into glasses. Somehow Henry Mancini's lush *101 Strings* playing *Moon River* had crept into the queue. This was a spiritual moment. Nothing else was necessary for her survival. Juliet, who usually treasured and protected her golden-hued world-view, actually admitted that something was wrong. This was important information.

"I know Tuscany is probably mythical, but it works for me," Juliet said.

They each picked up a glass.

Raphael held his glass out in a toast. "To placebos," he said.

Sabine took a sip. "A placebo isn't really a placebo if it works."

"Everything is a placebo," Raphael said.

"That's why this whole balance is so very fragile," Juliet said. "On the one hand I know Paris may be hallucinatory, but on the other hand I believe it wholeheartedly because that's the only way it's going to work."

"What does this mean in terms of decrypting these files?" Sabine said.

"So, yeah, about Tristan," Raphael said.

"I feel an event horizon coming up," Juliet said. "It's a little off-centering."

"And Clea is out of the psych ward and roaming the streets," said Sabine.

"My colleagues at *The Village Voice* all have gone on to write important books," said Raphael.

"When I go on walks I feel a psychotic break with reality. And is that really such a bad thing?" said Juliet.

"I say no," said Raphael. "Not if it brings you peace of mind."

"He's right," said Sabine. "Especially if you dissociate."

There was a long silence while everyone took many thoughtful sips of their wine. This was far more satisfying than Henry's files.

"In answer to your question, Raphael," said Juliet, "My husband has been very sick. He insists on keeping his travel schedule, though, and that's put his chemotherapy protocol out of whack. I'm not sure which is better – putting your life on hold and living longer, or living your life fully and dying sooner. That's our marital issue right now."

Sabine gave Raphael a look that said "Top that," whereupon Raphael silently shuffled through the files.

A few moments passed as Juliet and Sabine watched the papers move around the coffee table. Then Juliet put her wine glass down and said "Wait!"

Raphael and Sabine looked up.

"There's something there." She pointed at a file.

Sabine plucked the piece of paper Juliet was pointing to. She leaned back and read aloud from a handwritten note in the margin:

Life is...

Jazz singer Mark Murphy had rotated to the front of Juliet's Pandora shuffle. His rough-cut baritone was lamenting the loss of his home city as he began a road trip down I-95, in Richie Cole's song *D.C. Farewell.* "The dream has passed," he sang. Sabine noted that he didn't say "the dream is gone." He said "the dream has passed." So the dream is merely transient, that's all. Moving continuously. Sabine's life as a Manhattan ex-pat living in Trauma Town pining after a disembodied male voice on a police scanner could simply be a dynamic part of something. Perhaps she just had to push it along to see what the big picture might turn out to be.

Juliet interrupted the confused silence. "I'm a grandmother."

"Yes I know," Sabine said. "I am too actually."

The two women looked at Raphael. "I'm only 45," he said as if he had been accused. "But. You never know where life on the multiverse might take you, am I right?" He padded to the door and put on his large boots. "Gotta go write newspaper copy."

Raphael closed the door behind him.

"Funny he should mention the multiverse," Juliet said. "I was just thinking about that."

"Odd how there are so many connections across different dimensions." Sabine thought that was an appropriate response. She was proud of herself for fitting in. "Clea said something about a grandmother and a document when she shot Denize last month."

"Really? Denize said something about a grandmother and a document when I visited her at her rehab!" Juliet said as if hitting on something extraordinary.

Sabine moved from the floor to the couch. "How did you know Denize, anyway. I was surprised to see you there."

"I got a call that she wanted to see me. I didn't know her before that, although…"

"What."

Juliet shrugged her shoulders.

"Can I speak to a treason nurse?"

"Umm." Sabine adjusted her headset. She was happy at her workstation in the switchboard room. The fire panel was beeping, but it hadn't gone into a full, strobe-lit Code Red, so she ignored it. "A treason nurse?"

"Yes, in the emergency room."

"Oh. You mean a *triage* nurse. Yes, hold while I transfer you." The actual treason nurse is out in the parking lot with the firing squad, Sabine mumbled.

"No gun talk," said Glo without looking up from her computer screen. "This is the switchboard, what can I do for you?... You have a procedure tomorrow and you need to know what time?... Okay, Sir," Glo said, "Wow, unfortunately I can't help you. My database software isn't working and it's 11:30 at night, so no one who's here knows anything either... What kind of procedure are you getting tomorrow?...You don't know? Okay, well who is your doctor?... You're not sure? Okay, hmm, I mean, are you coming in for like an x-ray? A blood draw? A colonoscopy? A flu shot? Heart surgery?... You forgot to write it down? Okay, don't panic, everything's okay, I promise, we're just two people figuring it all out, okay Sir?... Now. What's wrong with you – do you have a disease? A broken bone? A brain tumor?...Not sure, okay..."

Sabine clicked onto her next call.

"I'm in Room 220. I need you to call the police."

"What's going on?" Sabine said.

"My television doesn't get the Boomerang Channel."

"Hold while I transfer you to the nurse's station."

"No! I don't want the nurse. I want the TV fixed."

"The nurse arranges that, so ..."

"The nurse hates me. I want the police."

"Your nurse has a pipeline to maintenance, I promise."

"No she doesn't. I already asked her. Get me the president."

"Administration won't be in until tomorrow morning."

"No, of the United States."

"Oh."

"I'm an amputee and I want to speak to the president of the United States."

"Hold for just a second, okay?" Sabine held her left earphone away from her head. "Glo."

"Epilepsy? E coli?" Glo put her caller on mute. "What."

"How deeply into a patient's psychosis are we supposed to go?" Sabine said.

"Our patients are our customers."

"He wants the president of the United States."

"Put him through to the White House. Duh." Glo unmuted her call. "Was it maybe a tapeworm?"

Sabine put her earphone back on, Googled the phone number for the White House, and transferred the call.

Aja came into the switchboard room with an audible 'It's cold out there but toasty in here' sigh. She hung her faux fur, vintage-look Hell Bunny coat on the back of the door, over Sabine's and Glo's coats that were jammed on the one hook. All the coats fell to the floor. Aja picked them up and got them to stay on the hook. The December chill clung to her as she brushed by Glo and Sabine and plopped down at her work station.

Glo was still trying to help her caller figure out why he was supposed to report to the hospital tomorrow. If indeed it was the hospital he was to report to. And if it was tomorrow. "Flesh-eating bacterial infection?...No, um – oh wait, let me put you through to our specialist." She put the caller on hold. "Aja – line 3 for you."

"Glo, for Godsake," Sabine said. "She just started her shift. It'll throw her into her fried brain spasms. She's young yet."

"I'm right here," Aja said. "I can handle it, lay it on me. My mom just made me a ginseng smoothie."

"Okay, stand by," said Glo. Then while clicking her keyboard, "So Sabine, did you figure out what Henry Moho wants you to do with those manila files?"

"I have my people working on it," Sabine said.

"Oh good," Glo said. "You, your crazy neighbor, and the Pleiades. Should be resolved in no time. In the meantime, I heard through the intel vine that Henry is this close to disintegrating our department entirely and having the hospital phones answered by robots."

"I know, Glo," Sabine said. "But his files are incoherent, and even if I decrypted them I'm not sure it would have useful information."

"Every tiny piece of intel is useful, Sabine. Each little nano-threadlette of subatomic mini-knowledge has value. I'm using Juliet-speak here, so you'll understand me."

"I'm sorry, Sir," Aja said into her headset. "My database won't boot up. Then we have midnight going on, so the only signs of life here are us operators and the nurses in the emergency room. You don't remember what they're supposed to do to you tomorrow?"... Was it an x-ray perhaps? A blood draw? A dialysis treatment?" Her voice was young, like a millennial. Sincere. "So okay, like, are you sick? Did you fall and break a bone? Fracture your skull?"

Sabine clicked on "new call" and dialed Juliet's cell phone. "Can you get down here right now?"

"Yes, okay, sure. Just a minute, though, I'm in the middle of Patti Lupone's Fantine singing 'I Dreamed a Dream'. It always blows me away. Somehow I feel the need to be blown away. What's up?"

"I love *Les Mis*, I've always meant to see it." A pause to affect sincerity. "Okay, so call Raphael and have him come in, too. We need to get this thing happening before the end of the world kicks in."

"Sweetie. End of the world? I'm all over it. Be right there."

With wet winter coats piled on the empty engineer's desk in the back of the dark switchboard room and puddles by the door where boots had been peeled off and left, Sabine, Glo, Juliet, and Raphael sat around the two front work stations. Aja stayed at her station behind them, to answer phones.

"Tell me again why this matters?" said Raphael.

"Because we're giving you an exclusive on the story," Sabine said.

"Oh yes, the story," Raphael said. "What story?" He looked at Glo. "You!"

"Yes. Sorry I said 'fuck you' to you on the phone," Glo answered. "But here's the angle for your story. People who come into the hospital are furious. They are beyond upset, they are super-mega cortisol-challenged."

"I wasn't that upset when they brought me in to the ER," Juliet said. "They were very nice, actually."

"That's because you put out your own nice energy, Juliet," Aja called from her workstation. "You have good emergency room karma."

"That's because you were unconscious," Glo corrected.

Juliet smiled. She was wearing lingerie, because it was the middle of the night and Trummel shut down at 6 pm so the entire town was basically hers. Not that there was anything in it to have, but running around in her lingerie, she told Sabine, was a good way to float on a certain gossamer energy that she found useful at times. "Thank you, Aja," she said.

"What Glo means," Sabine said, "is that everyone's upset, no one knows anything, and no one tells anyone anything and no one is accountable."

"So?" Raphael said.

"Although we push computer buttons here in the switchboard room," Sabine continued, "seldom do people actually connect. They almost always get some monster-elongated automated phone answering tree that would make you want to jump off a bridge rather than be bored to death listening to the options, but even after they choose their extension, they are then met with more automated message choices and finally a voice mail because in the end there's no one at the other end. Ever."

"We're asking for bullet-proof windows in here," Glo said.

Raphael looked around him. "What windows."

"Yesterday," Glo continued unabated, "the entire orthopedic floor's phones were answered with an automated answering tree that said the hospital was closed for spring break. All the back lines, too."

"It's December," said Juliet.

"We figured it out!" Aja shouted. "Oh, sorry, Sir, I just got so excited. You're welcome!" She turned to face the others. "He wasn't sick – that's why he didn't know what was wrong with him. It's his wife who's coming in for a procedure! Oh thank goodness, I helped somebody today."

"What's wrong with his wife?" asked Glo.

"He has no idea, but he was over it and hung up."

"Was he mad?" asked Raphael.

"Why, no, no he thanked me," Aja said. "That's why I love my job. I get to be of service." Aja's left eye snapped shut as her head jerked to the left.

Suddenly the Code Phone pierced the dark little room with its whooping ringtone and blue strobe lights. Aja grabbed the call faster than an EMT pushing a defibrillator *on* button, but her trained voice came out like the lazy steam from a hot apple pie sitting in a sunny Midwestern window. "Code Phone," she said with full-on cool. "Why certainly, no problem." She punched up another number and grabbed the microphone. Her assured, enunciating voice went out on the hospital-wide overhead. "Attention all personnel,

Code Silver." Her right eye snapped shut and stayed that way. "Attention all personnel, Code Silver."

"Good thing we have bullet proof – um, walls," said Glo.

"What's a Code Silver again?" said Juliet.

"It's a person with a gun," mumbled Raphael.

"Switchboard to Security," Sabine said into the radio.

"Security. Go ahead Switchboard." said Victor.

"Did you copy the Code Silver?"

"Affirmative."

Sabine pushed the talk button. "What's going on, Victor?"

"No idea, Sabine."

Sabine put the radio down as Glo picked up a red landline that went directly to 911. Glo purred into the hotline with the smoothness of mission control. "Yes, Officer, we're experiencing a Code Silver at this time. Yes. Thank you. You're welcome." A little laugh. "You too."

"What did they say?" Juliet asked.

"Nothing," Glo said.

Sabine was on her computer preparing an MCI blast page, a Mass Casualty Incident beeper page, to go out to the hospital administration. They would undoubtedly be upset – not so much about the Code

Silver, because they would assume it to be a false alarm, but because it was the middle of the night.

Juliet stood up. "I'm not dressed for this," she said, alarmed.

"Hello, Steve from the lab," Aja said into her headset. "What's up?...So tell your radiation safety officer that your dosimeter fell into your soup at lunch. They'll fix it, it's their job. You're welcome"

"You can't leave now, Juliet," Sabine said. "Code Silver means we shelter in place. Preferably hide under the desks. Someone will give us the all clear and then we'll announce that, and then it's over except for writing a hundred reports."

"I don't know that they clean under there," Juliet whispered, glancing under Sabine's desk.

"Nonsense," Glo said. "They cleaned under the desks just last year. Wait, was it the year before –"

There was heavy pounding on the switchboard room door.

"It's Nyx," Sabine said."

"We don't know that," Raphael said.

"It's *Exotic Nights* by Avon for Godsake," said Sabine. She stood up and unattached herself from her headset cord. "Open the door, Raphael, she's standing in the damn hallway."

Raphael rushed to the door, unlocked it, and Nyx rushed in. "I hate this place," she said, then looked up at Raphael who had just locked the door after her. "Oh, hi there."

"Hi." Raphael smiled. "You're gorgeous."

Nyx visibly relaxed. "Thank you."

"I'm a writer."

"Oh!"

"Yes, and a journalist. Working on a front page story."

"Well. A little bit of class here at Trauma Town. Nice work, ladies, where did you find him?" Nyx said.

More pounding on the door. Raphael turned to Sabine. "What does your perfume radar tell you now?"

"Nothing," Sabine said. "But I don't think a mass murderer would, like, knock on the door, right?"

"There was someone behind me," Nyx said. "Maybe they're stranded in the hall, too. Everyone has their doors locked."

"I'm getting a signal from somewhere," Juliet said.

Nyx turned to Juliet and her eyes lit up. "Nice nightgown."

Juliet smiled. "Oh thank you. It's from Paris. Chanel."

Nyx sank into Sabine's desk chair. "Really?"

"What kind of signal are you getting," Glo asked Juliet. Given that no one knew if the code was a false alarm, a drill, or even real, and Nyx didn't know anything, the scanner had gone dark, and Security was at the other end of the radio waves, which could be anywhere, Glo decided that any intel Juliet could get from any parallel universe would be better than what they had.

"It's a really bad feeling," Juliet said. "And it's impending."

Nyx got up and ran to the door. "We'd better let them in then." She unlocked it.

"Don't open the door," Juliet said.

Nyx opened the door. Clea stood in the entrance, her frizzy red hair wilder than Sabine remembered. She was wearing a short, baggy dress and high heels, and in her shaking hands was a pistol.

Chapter 11

The thought drifted through Sabine's mind:
I feel safer dead than I ever did when I was alive.
Except ... what about the cats.

A loud pop jolted the switchboard room, but mostly Sabine heard nothing – just suddenly she felt her desk slam into the side of her face. Her mousepad smelled of Avon Hawaii Nights hand cream. Then she heard the distant sound of someone in her headset saying, *"Is it true they have Whoopie Pies for $2.00 in the cafeteria today?"*. And then nothing. Blackness. And then off in the distance, across a wide lake, she was crawling across a shaking rope bridge. She remembered Juliet's comment from a month ago when Juliet first woke up in the emergency room: "Was that a dream? It felt so real."

Then, just like that, Sabine was underneath the streets of Manhattan's far west side, waiting in the near-dark for a train. There was a question about which train to take. She knew at one time, but now they weren't marked. She asked someone if the train that was pulling in was going to ... And then she couldn't remember where she was supposed to go, so she was driving a car, going up the entrance ramp in an unfamiliar suburban tree-less interstate cloverleaf.

"Take a right here," said the man in the passenger seat. "And get onto I 95 North."

"Wow, you look like -" Sabine said.

"But you must watch the road so you don't get us killed, yes?" He had the hint of a French accent, but it wasn't Parisian French like Sabine learned in high school, it had more of a Hungarian influence.

Sabine merged onto the deserted highway.

The man was in his handsome mid-fifties, and there was the tiniest sparkle in his eyes. Sabine couldn't place him. "You look like... I think I saw your photo..."

And then she was walking by herself through a busy downtown hotel, looking for the bar. It struck her that sitting with a nice glass of Merlot would be perfect right now. She had a room at this hotel, so she could go freshen up anytime she wanted. But the place was enormous. In fact it was connected to another building where there were busy restaurants, a choral music performance on a stage in a huge auditorium, cute little souvenir shops, dance recitals, warm and inviting nightclubs, dorm rooms, a tiny restaurant with sparkling party lights strung across the entrance, and bistro tables in the hall. The hall was also an outdoor sidewalk café – all indoors in this underground city hub by the hotel.

"If I can sit at a little round table with a glass of wine and listen to a mellow jazz trio, I can be eternally happy," Sabine whispered to the French/Hungarian guy.

He opened the door to a packed lounge, which was a converted cafeteria. There was an empty stage in the back, with a sound system, microphones and a drum set. It was early, perhaps around six p.m. "Don't stay too long, Sabine," he said. "You have someplace you need to be."

Clea shrieked and dropped her pistol. Before the echo from the gunshot even stopped, Glo was all over the radio. "Code Silver in Telecomm, stat."

"*Telecomm*?" a male voice answered.

"The switchboard room? Basement Level 2. Jesus."

Aja leapt to the microphone and paged overhead "Attention all personnel. Rapid Response, Telecommunications. Rapid Response, Telecommunications."

Juliet took off her beige satin bathrobe and put it over a slumped Sabine. It instantly turned red. Blood was seeping into Sabine's computer.

Clea was on the floor in the corner by the door hinges, watching the action as if stunned.

Raphael materialized a phone and was taking pictures.

Someone running in high heels came down the hall toward the switchboard room. Yanina, the Utilization Review nurse, appeared in the doorway, her cell phone attached to her ear by a raised shoulder, and a laptop in her hands. "I can't talk right now, Maz ---- no, I'm not trying to avoid you, although I would if I were, but --- no, your insurance company is not going to cover your stroke – no, you're not covered for rehab either. No coverage, nothing I can do about it."

"Yunky, call 911," Glo said to Yanina. "Sabine's been shot."

"That's really a lot of blood," Yanina said.

"Yunky!"

"911? Yes, we have a shooting here at the hospital in Telecomm. It's the 2nd basement level. The shooter?" Yanina looked around the room. Clea was still on the floor in the corner, with no one paying attention to her. "I don't know, he's not here. Yes, I would assume the hospital is on lockdown but who really knows. You think your insurance company will pay for your stroke, but it's all the turn of the Big Wheel."

The Rapid Response team arrived – two paramedics ("Damn, Sabine," Glo muttered. "What good is getting shot if you can't see the handsome hunks that have come to save you?"), a tech wheeling a gurney, and Lulu from the ER. The cave had come alive. Lulu led the charge as she and the paramedics carried Sabine from her desk to the gurney.

"It's going to be okay," Lulu said. "It looks like the bullet grazed her forehead. I don't think it … went in."

"I hear you. The body flashes into and out of this dimension at a speed so fast, we think we're only in this one place," Juliet said to Lulu, as if hoping Lulu might be able to use this information. "I was a nurse in Vietnam."

Nyx backed off in horror, breathing hard, and bumped into Clea. "Be careful, Lulu!" Nyx shouted. "Sabine hates for people to mess with her hair." She looked at Raphael, standing next to her, and suddenly slapped the phone out of his hand. It landed on the floor. "Damn paparazzi," she said.

"What. The public has a right to know." Raphael picked up his phone. "This is what Sabine would want."

"You sound like the Long Island Medium," Glo said. "You have no idea what Sabine would want. Only I know what Sabine would want."

"She's going to be fine!" shouted Lulu. "Honest to freaking God." They had Sabine on the gurney, but couldn't get a pathway out of the tiny room. "If we can ever get her out of here."

"Everybody please move out of the freaking way," Glo shouted.

"There's no where to move," Aja apologized, backing up into Yanina.

"Oxford Healthcare won't cover this," Yanina said. "Aetna might, though, as a secondary."

The handsome scanner voice said, *"Shooting at the hospital, Lower Level 2, Telecomm, Delta Level. Shooting at the hospital, Delta Level. 0220,"* as smoothly as if he were announcing a gate change at the airport.

"I can't get the damn door unlocked," said Nyx.

Aja's head ticked to the left. "It's the end of the world here, am I the only one who sees this?" Her right eye had opened, but her left eye snapped shut. "It's not true that a whole bunch of clowns can fit into one phone booth. My head hurts. I mean mostly Sabine's head must hurt. I'm guilty, I admit it. My complacency caused the Vietnam war. My mother was right. Although I don't think I was born yet."

Juliet perked up. "End times!" she said as if a difficult puzzle piece had just slid into place, making all the surrounding pieces suddenly recognizable as a coherent picture. Then she composed herself, perhaps realizing that to communicate with earth people one had to speak low and slow. She smiled enigmatically. Her voice went velvet and breathy. "But remember, dearest young Aja, life doesn't end with the physical body. End times or not, our real selves are formless. I think."

Raphael whispered into Juliet's ear. "This may not be the best time to bring up the afterlife. I think we need to stay positive." Sweat dripped down his forehead, and his voice shook. "You know, positive. Like, positive energy."

"Yes of course," Juliet whispered back to him. "I'm just saying. This earth-bound side is dense and hard to move around in. Like trying to walk underwater. The other side is light and free. You're still you, you can just kind of do more stuff without as much hassle."

"I understand that the transportation system is better over there," Raphael said. "But if Sabine goes there, that means she's… you know, not here. This would disrupt my script and make me wonder about pre-destination." Raphael looked around. "Where is Clea?"

Sinking into a soft, red velvet couch in her uptown hotel lobby, Sabine had her cell phone in her hand. As she looked down at it, it started to demolecularize, StarTrek transporter style. "No, I don't want to lose my phone," she said out loud. The phone became solid again. She clicked on *911* and put it to her ear. No answer. She hung up and clicked on *911* again. A voice on the other end explained that she was out of reach. Then the phone dematerialized completely. "I hate when that happens," she thought.

"These damn end times," Tristan said, next to her on the couch, in his Hungarian-French accent. "I've never been able to get a phone connection from here."

Sabine smiled in sudden recognition. "You're Juliet's husband!" She realized she looked gorgeous, as a friend of Juliet's should, with her shoulder-length silky brunette hair and straight bangs. She was glad she had gone full maquillage that morning, with her matte suede Clinique Moonlit-beige eyeshadow and smoky black liner. Surely Juliet's husband would approve of their friendship.

"And I'm actually not here," Tristan said. "As you're actually not here."

"I'm here, I am actually here."

"But I mean, we're both kind of hanging on. Undecided." Tristan was smashingly handsome in a ruggedly disheveled but acceptably European way. Deep wrinkles and graying temples validated his sophic eyes. Dark, spikey hair made him look nicely tortured, as if he hadn't slept in quite some time. He wore a black suit with a loosened skinny tie from 1974.

Sabine felt a chill down her back as she realized that he and Juliet made the perfect couple. "Hanging on?"

Two young guys in sweats and sneakers, carrying racquets, walked by the red velvet couch in the long hall where Sabine and Tristan were sitting. The soft, recessed lighting from some sort of overhead glow, made the boys look a little translucent; not quite solid. "You have an ulcer?!" said the smaller boy. He had red cheeks. "Really? I have a hiated hernia!!!"

Gentle, piped-in music permeated the hallway, and filled it with a luxurious string-wash of harmonic loveliness. Sabine vaguely recognized it as the *Succulent Chilled Beats* station she had discovered the night before, while trying yet again to sleep.

"We're hanging on, Sabine," Tristan continued. "Clinging to life. For various reasons."

"You because you love Juliet, right? You can't bear to leave her?"

"I've always loved her, but that's not it." Tristan took a deep breath, loosened his already loose black skinny tie, and crossed his legs. "It's that if I move through the tunnel to the next level, I'll be out of range, and Juliet will go under."

"I sense that that's true. I knew she was hanging on to something, I didn't know it was you."

"It's me. And honestly, the white light is calling me. My mom and dad are there. But what can you do? I can't let Juliet sink into a world of crippling delusion."

"I don't know, Tristan. She kind of already is in a world of, well, of her own."

Tristan seemed to shrink in size.

"She thinks you are alive and living in your condo," Sabine said. "She thinks you're traveling, doing lectures."

"I am."

"I can see that, Tristan. But hello, you're not all that accessible, right?"

"Okay, I admit it, I'm dead. So now I'm supposed to be wise and patient. But I can't wait to get out of here, Sabine. That's why I'm here with you on your little journey."

"So, say what?"

"My hope is that you'll look after Juliet so I don't have to. You're still slated to go back to earth, whatever that actually is. I'm needing to move on before I lose my mind, but I'm needing someone to watch out for her. Her granddaughter is in Budapest with a Hungarian lover. Juliet has no one."

"But Tristan, she loves you. She is an innocent."

"I know, Sabine, but things change. Death parted us. My contract has been fulfilled."

Sabine stared at Tristan for a few seconds, trying to get a grasp on the situation. "Here's the thing," she finally said. "I'm not so sure I want to go back. I mean I will because of my cats, but it's just not safe over there."

"And what else?" Tristan said.

"Well and also there's –." She looked at him, distressed.

"You can say it. No one will hear you, we're in some sort of hallucination."

"Okay then." A large orange tabby cat jumped into Sabine's lap. She stroked him. He purred loudly. "I'm hanging on because I'm still looking for home."

Victor bashed into the door to Telecomm with his solid, robust shoulder. Because it was already opened, it fell off its hinges and smashed into the already crowded room. Eusebio was right behind him, with Tom from Plant and Bill from Biomed. "Is Sabine okay?" he shouted over the reverberations of the smashing door, the undercurrent of Glo, Aja, Yanina, Nyx, Juliet and Raphael madly figuring out how and why the world works as it does, and the fire alarm now whooping.

Tom from Plant had recently installed a Hugs 'N Kisses security alarm in the Labor and Delivery unit.

The newborns' wristbands were coded so that if anyone attempted a kidnapping, Security and Switchboard would be alerted. Now, however, its high-pitched alarm screeched from all three operators' switchboards, with a message flashing across the screens saying "System Malfunction/False Alarm". As Aja called Labor and Delivery to make sure all the babies were okay, a deluge of calls came into the switchboard from the automated email blast that the Hugs 'N Kisses program sent out.

"I called 911!" said Yanina.

"You don't need them, Yunky," said Eusebio, harried and annoyed. "We're here and we're certified."

"It's just a graze, she'll be fine," Lulu shouted back, "if I could get this gurney out of here and into the emergency room where we have life-saving equipment."

Clea burst into loud sobbing tears, got up off the floor in front of the broken door, and ran to Victor. "Victor! You have to help me. Something terrible has happened."

Victor, freshly invigorated from a recent online refresher course in active shooter response, opened his burly arms to take in the small creature.

"I can't do this, Victor," Clea said. Her red, frizzy curls caught in the tears running down her pale, freckled face. "The gun went off. It was out of my control."

"Alright, everyone quiet," Victor yelled. Then softly to Clea, "Have they been bullying you again?"

"I'm on the verge," Clea whispered in Victor's ear.

"Alright, just stay with me, I got this." Victor stroked her hair, almost in a trance, as if remembering some moment from his own past, his own daughter, his own hidden story.

Glo moved to the dismembered door and pushed its remains further out of the way. "Lulu, look, we can get the gurney out. Hey! Will everyone get out of the freaking way?"

"Suggestion. Let's all move out into the hall," Nyx yelled over the still shrieking baby alarm.

"The hall," echoed Juliet.

"Into the hall, people," Raphael clarified.

A mass exodus followed, and then, finally, Lulu and the paramedics were able to push the gurney out of the tiny dark office. Sabine's pale face flashed alternately green and red, reflecting the room's now haywire digital lights.

The hallway itself seemed far safer because the fluorescent lighting, the muddy-yellow walls, and the worn, stained low-pile industrial carpet gave off a feeling of everyday normalcy. Bad things never happened in dependable fluorescent-lit normalcy.

Sabine grabbed her wine glass and got up from her cozy little café table. She was enjoying the party atmosphere with the party lights strung across the courtyard hallway, but Tristan and the orange tabby were gone, and she realized she had an important meeting to attend.

She walked with purpose down the softly lit, marbled hallway. Her five-inch heels clicked neatly as she glided toward the conference room. She loved her shoes. When she got to the conference room she realized she also had on a flowing golden ball gown and tons of makeup. Her hands were smooth, with long red fingernails - the ugly blue veins and sunspots were gone - and her wrists were adorned with Alex and Ani bracelets.

In the conference room, everyone was already seated. They were chatting casually as Sabine sat at the empty chair at the head of the long, glass oblong table. In front of each person was a huge glass of exquisite white wine filled to the brim, with pastel sparkles reflecting gently through the Tiffany glassware. Muted music played in the background. Sabine recognized it as Ramsey Lewis' jazz classic

The In Crowd from her Pandora station *DeepHouse VibeOut*. The room became quiet.

"Welcome, Sabine," said Counselor Deanna Troi in her Betazoid accent.

Sabine felt safe. Counselor Troi was her favorite *Star Trek Next Gen* person. Just hearing the even, lux-velvet timbre of Counselor Troi's voice made Sabine feel that nothing bad could ever happen. Kind of like Juliet's voice.

Juliet. The planet earth: the self-contained switchboard room, her pink Trauma Town Dispatch hoodie, her gaggle of warm kitties, her deep, safe cave where she spoke to invisible needy people and helped them find their way through the hospital maze. The memory of earth took on a liquid dreamy quality.

As she thought about where Juliet might be in all this, she sensed a commotion going on above her. People running around in circles, pushing gurneys into emergency rooms, pulling their hair out, sitting on linoleum kitchen floors sobbing into bottles of Johnny Walker Black. She remembered the fragments of a dream – something about a file on her because she helped a teenager in an elevator – so meaningless, yet in the dream it seemed so important.

"Are we on the Enterprise?" Sabine asked. "Did I die and go to the Enterprise?"

"Maybe, maybe not," said Deanna Troi. "How does that make you feel?"

"Okay I think, maybe."

Sabine looked at her companions. Counselor Troi was on her immediate left. Next to her was Julian Boulevard, who was the death on Three the day Glo was throwing up. "I heard you were coming," Julian said. "I just wanted to say thank you to you for making sure they knew not to use the DNR until my wife could get there to say goodbye. That was huge, Sabine."

"Oh, it was my pleasure," Sabine replied, and then quickly wondered what a better response might have been.

Next to Julian, Swami Vivekananda was burning Nag Champa incense, which reminded her of Manhattan's 92nd Street Y where she met her first husband.

Opposite Sabine on the other side of the long glass table was Sherri from HR. She looked conciliatory. "They only gave me a second, because I told them it was important, but I do have to go back. We're prepared to offer you a large lump sum - but you need to sign the bottom where it says you won't sue us."

"Oh. Thank you, Sherri, um, yeah, I guess, well maybe. I kind of have stuff on my mind right now but I'll totally, um. What?"

On the other end of the oblong table, were, of all people, Maz and Dave from the Trummel Rehab Center - the guys she met when she went to visit Denize. There had evidently been a helicopter crash as they were going from Trummel to Cincinnati. Maz had had another stroke, and, without the availability of a Medflight, Dave had commissioned an uber copter which had crashed into Mount Monadnock.

Alfonso Brown and Sister Sadie from Eddie Jefferson's 1961 album The Jazz Singer popped in, apparently to see if this was where they were supposed to be, said "Oops," and then quickly left.

When everyone was quiet, Maz stood up and addressed the group. "Hi. I'm Maz and I'm in a coma," he said.

"Hi, Maz," mumbled everyone.

"I don't think I'm actually dead yet though."

"Way to go, Maz," someone said.

"And I'm Dave," announced Dave. "Maz's number was up, and I just happened to be on the same helicopter."

"Sorry about that, Dave," said Maz. "My number must have overridden your number."

Next to Maz and Dave, under the soft recessed lights, Sabine was surprised to see Jeanette from The Accordion Connection across the street from The Black

Cat. She had apparently been electrocuted while repairing an accordion during a severe thunderstorm. "Does anyone know where the music room is?" she asked. "I may be lost, I'm not sure."

"We have no provisions for a music room," said Volt from HR, next to her, who passed away before the hospital was built, but couldn't let go. Volt had pioneered the concept of employee-centered human resources, combining pop psychology with random algorhythms and paid rehab time. He was before his time, and left the planet an unfulfilled man. "But you're welcome to stay here until someone comes for you."

"Thank you so much," said Jeanette, "I'm okay, it's all good, I just needed someone to -" she blinked back tears. "To -"

"I know, dear," said Volt. "I know."

Jeanette picked up a stack of accordion music and tiptoed out of the room.

And then Sabine locked eyes with a gorgeous older woman at the opposite end of the oblong table. The woman's eyes sparkled with recognition, and Sabine was struck with the same feeling of connection as when she first saw Denize in elevator 2.

The woman was stunning, with platinum white shoulder-length hair, straightened in a perfect bob, flawless pale skin with deep wrinkles, black eyeliner and mascara, and the perfect shade of red lipstick. You can't get that shade on earth. Matte finish, not too dark, not too orange but not too blue-based. She wore a deep blue gown with a floor-length tiered satin skirt.

"Sabine." Her voice was deep and slightly textured with the distant hint of foreign whisky and exotic cigarettes – and the trace of an accent – might it be French? Hungarian? "Sabine. I'm Juliet's third great-grandmother, on the Indigo side."

"Oh!" Sabine felt a surge of happiness, intrigue, and privilege wash over her. Juliet was her hero. That Juliet's third great grandmother would even know her name made her feel like royalty from a distant planet. "I'm honored," she whispered.

Grandmother Indigo smiled. "I know, dear. But we have more important things going on right now."

"Yes," said Sabine. The others around the table nodded in agreement. Stuff was important. Chaos reigned. Was there a pattern in the fabric? "Um, what?"

A distant but handsome male voice echoed in a faraway static as if on a police scanner. *"Signal 22. Trauma Town Emergency room. Signal 22."*

Sabine got lost in a moment. A distant memory - or was it just a wish - of a capable hero, perhaps in a uniform, who saved lives, rescued dogs from cisterns, delivered the occasional baby, resuscitated shark attack victims, and fearlessly drove ambulances through red lights with sirens blaring.

Signal 22. Sabine returned to the present moment. "Oh no, you guys. Signal 22 is code for a dead body," she said to the group. Then, reflexively, she looked around for her 2-way radio so she could notify Lulu in the ER that a body was coming into the morgue. In the corner of her eye she thought she saw Henry Moho through the glass doors of the conference room, standing in the muted, warm glow of the soothing, softly lit hallway. But the moment she turned her head to see for sure, he was gone.

Simultaneously, in a different, more dense and heavy reality, Operator Glo was saying "What's the prognosis, Lulu?"

Raphael was talking into his phone. "Trauma Town. Where the world collides with the... Where collisions occur... Trauma Town... shit.... Lulu, how is she doing? Do you guys capitalize the E and the D when you write Emergency Department?"

Juliet said, "I just saw *The Hunt for Dark Matter* on YouTube and I'm wondering if this could have something to do with MACHO – Massive Compact Halo Objects – that may be invisibly permeating the universe. This could have been what happened to Sabine"

"No way to tell," Lulu said. "Our radiology department is still earth-bound. Wait, Henry? Henry Moho? What are you doing here? You look ill."

Glo jerked her head around to where Lulu was looking. "Henry? I don't see him, Lulu." Then she spoke really loud, turning a slow circle. "Henry wherever you are, this totally is not an Incident, okay?"

Yanina from Utilization Review pushed her short gray hair back, away from her eyes, and secured it on top of her head with her glasses. "I have no P & P for this. The best I can do is work-related injury, but Trauma Town has been having a little misunderstanding with the Department of Labor."

Nyx said, "I almost could have prevented this. I was like a day away from getting clearance to gather intel in the Program Unit Facility. I feel like I've failed at my job, and Sabine has paid the price."

Aja, inspired, was all over that. "We mustn't blame ourselves, Nyx. We need to channel our energies into a group, um, channel."

Clea, who had moved with the group to the ER, had slid from Victor to Raphael, and was sobbing into Raphael's arms. Raphael knew who she was, and held his breath. If he didn't make any sharp movements or jolt the universal workings, perhaps now he could get

198 / Suzann Kalehis story for the paper, straight from the shooter's mouth.

Yanina's glasses fell off her head. "People! People - who's answering the phones and dispatching the ambulances?"

Glo and Aja exchanged glances.

"Oh God," Aja said.

"The automated answering system tree," Glo said. "Bill from Biomed programmed it to answer after four rings. It's never been tested."

Glo, Aja, Sabine, and Valentine, Tashuna, and Wing all prided themselves on being able to pick up a call on the half of the first ring while simultaneously triaging ambulance runs, silencing fire panel false alarms, overhead paging the various catastrophes, and connecting the correct people to their appropriate traumas. The operators were fast and focused. Just yesterday Glo and Sabine had a race to see who could handle all five of their phone lines without losing a call. "Hospital, can you hold please?" Click. "Hospital, can you hold please?" Click. "Thank you for holding, how can I direct your call?" Click. "Thank you for holding, how can I direct your call."

The sea of people parted as Dr. Raj pushed through them and into the small exam room. "Lulu, call the switchboard, we need the brain surgeon on call, stat."

"I have this, Doctor," Glo screamed. She ran out of the exam room and over to the ER registration desk behind which the on-call doctors were listed on a chalkboard. "We don't have a brain surgeon!" she yelled back.

"Find one," Dr. Raj shrieked. "We don't have time for a med flight."

"I'm paging Dr. Sam," Glo yelled. Dr. Sam was a family pediatrician, but he could do no wrong, even if his patients died, because he went to Doctors Without Borders every few months and Raphael had profiled him in the *Sun*.

In the glassy calm of the gray conference room, smooth jazz played softly and Grandmother Indigo's deep blue dress, which now had tiny, brilliant diamonds sewn into the bodice, cast sparkles around the room. Sabine noticed the floor-to-ceiling glass window, and glanced out at the glittering cityscape below and the starry night sky.

"Yes, dear, we all know what a Signal 22 is, but that was kind of you to explain anyway," said Grandmother Indigo in a monotone Jeanne Moreau voice. "Not a big issue to be sure. The quick stop on the planet is nothing compared to the vast freedom of before and after. We all think earth is it while we're

200 / Suzann Kale

there, but it's a quick moment packed with drama and then we can thankfully move on."

"But my cats," Sabine whispered.

"You're going back, they're fine. My great great granddaughter is taking care of them for you in the meantime. Which reminds me." Grandmother Indigo opened her beige Chanel tote and took out a paper file. She sighed with controlled impatience. "Henry's been trying to get this information to you, dear. You didn't have to come all the way here for it, you know."

Chapter 12

Sabine was influenced early on by a Maxfield Parish exhibit at the Guggenheim Museum shortly after the artist said he was done painting girls on rocks. Juliet's life was influenced early on by Max Planck talking to her through a Ouija Board affirming the non-existence of linear time.

Grandmother Indigo was gorgeous and in command, sitting at the head of the expansive oval glass conference table in a 19th century ivory silk evening gown. The recessed lighting and the golden glow from the floor-to-ceiling windows reflecting the city's - or, some city's - shimmering skyline - bounced off the gown's pearl beading.

Grandmother Indigo had accessorized the dress with 21st century 6-inch stilettos in patent leather red. The heel of each stiletto was decorated with a tiny red and black bow. "Juliet got them from me," she explained as Sabine stared in delighted shock.

"Juliet has those shoes? I haven't seen them."

"I am borrowing them from her. You know, don't you?"

"Yes, of course." A beat. "Know what?"

"None of this is random," said Grandmother Indigo. "It's all synchronistic. You and Juliet being neighbors? Or better yet – you and Juliet ending up in your godforsaken Trauma Town in the middle of nowhere? What are the odds, right?"

"Oh. Well now that you mention it."

"So you're deciphering Henry's files?"

"Oh, yes. Or trying to. How do you know Henry?"

"We go way back. Anyway, I gave the file for safekeeping to my sister, Sauvignon Blue. You may know her sixth great granddaughter Denize."

"Denize LeClair? Yes, I know Denize!"

"Yes of course dear, but anyway Henry intercepted it when Denize got shot."

"In a nutshell, then," interrupted Counselor Troi, who had been monitoring the situation.

"Okay. Here it is." Grandmother Indigo leaned in.

Maz and Dave leaned in.

Volt was working on a paper for *HR Today* called *The Myth and the Prime Midlife Crisis Group,* and leaned in without looking up from his tablet.

"Okay," Grandmother Indigo explained. "So. We are like ants." Then she leaned back in her chair. "Wait, not ants. Tardigrades. We are like tardigrades." She laughed to herself, then sighed, then took a sip of her wine. Sabine noticed that her lipstick did not come off on the glass.

This was the last thing Sabine remembered before she woke up in Post Op Recovery Room 1. She stared blankly at Lulu, who was taking her pulse, and she wondered if she was still in the sparkling gray, softly lit conference room. "A tardigrade?" she wondered aloud. "I'm sorry, Grandmother, I just don't understand about tardigrades."

"Hello, okay! Sabine, you're speaking. That's good. How do you feel?" Lulu, as always, cut through surface concerns to get down to bones and blood.

"Oh. Feeling. Okay, I'm feeling heavy," mumbled Sabine. "I feel like I weigh a thousand pounds. How do people do this?"

"Sabine, it's Lulu. You're in the recovery room."

Juliet was on the other side of Sabine's bed in the small, sterile room. "Sabine, it's Juliet. You're back on earth."

"On, I mean… on, like, earth? The place with dirt and bad lipstick colors?'

"Ah, good call, little neighbor, you're totally alive," said Juliet.

"Good work. You're okay." Lulu looked over her readers to make reassuring eye contact. "The bullet just grazed you … what I mean is, you're fine. Really. How do you feel?"

"I feel, um, actually I'm worried about my cats."

"I'm all over that," Juliet said. "I've been taking care of the flock and they're fine. They get it."

"Oh, okay, Juliet, I mean thank you. I wasn't sure I had enough cat food stashed away."

"You didn't, so I cooked for them."

"You cooked? For the cat pack?"

"Well, I found a bunch of stuff they liked. Yogurt and butter. They loved it, they're happy. One of them threw up."

"Dr. Crusher threw up?"

"Someone threw up."

"Okay, then." Sabine felt heavy earthly oxygen fill her physical lungs and make her dizzy. She knew from dispatching ambulances for patients with acute respiratory failure, that anything lung-related meant you were still alive.

Freddie Mercury, Higgs-Boson and Dr. Crusher must be okay, and Juliet was an angel from Heaven. It was starting to make sense.

Mainly, though, Sabine knew she was back on the gelatinous, spongy earth, slogging through the 3-dimensions, because everything was dense and separate and … clammy. Just looking around the recovery room made Sabine feel like she was trying to walk through heavy water. Putting her arm back by her side when Lulu was done with the blood pressure took a shocking amount of energy and will. She never realized how heavy an arm could be.

And then there was Lulu's stethoscope: a huge, isolated chunk of a barbaric remnant from a distant, long-ago way of life. Lulu's hair, which used to be a lustrous L'Oréal Preference brunette # 5G, now seemed 2-dimensional and opaque. Lulu's blue scrubs - today with pictures of cocker spaniels and hearts - had a vivid blackish-purple undertone that reminded Sabine of Tim Burton's *Alice in Wonderland.* And oh yes, the drugstore glasses. There didn't seem to be one pair of them on the other side.

Although Juliet was gorgeous no matter what dimension she inhabited, her earthly diamond stud earrings lacked the internal glitter that Juliet's Grandmother Indigo's earrings had.

And then there was breathing. Sabine remembered to be grateful for her physical, three-dimensional working body and the autonomic nervous system. Still, having to breathe in and out was suddenly cumbersome.

"Then I feel okay, thanks Lulu," Sabine said.

Now, though, she viscerally understood what Juliet meant when she woke up in the emergency room last month, and said of her dream, "But it seemed so real."

"Do you know what happened?" asked Lulu.

"I figured a bunch of stuff out," said Sabine.

"What did you figure out?"

"Is Juliet still here? I need to talk to her about her husband."

Lulu tilted her head down and looked at Sabine over the tops of her readers. "It seems like your brain is still in your head, we weren't all that sure when you first got shot."

"No worries, I'm here," whispered Juliet. Her voice was husky and a little hoarse, as if she had been crying. "We can talk later, okay? What do you need right now? Anything you want."

"Cuervo Margarita, rocks, no salt."

"Good choice, Sabine," said Lulu, "because salt is bad for you."

Nurse Sunami and a young patient care technician wheeled a post-op car accident into the recovery room across from Sabine. "He was legally blind, so he was supposed to drive very slowly," Nurse Sunami explained.

"Okay then, guys," said Sabine. "Wake me when the Cuervo comes." She dozed off from the anesthesia shadow.

"This is Operator Glo."

"It's me." Sabine had been recovering in her third floor room after her surgery, and after three days was bored our of her mind.

"Jesus, Girl, I've got work to do here. You can't be calling the switchboard every five seconds."

"I know, I just need another intel update from the Bridge. Have we had many Medflights? How are the boys from Valley Ambulance behaving? Are they still antsy to get the really good myocardial infarctions?"

"Sabine, you lonely thing, guess what you missed?"

"Um, death?"

"More important than that. You missed the hugest event possible. You know the handsome guy's voice on the police scanner?"

"Yeah?"

"He came into Telecomm yesterday!"

"What? No!"

"My dear, you have no idea. He had on a uniform and my goodness he completely met all my expectations of what a handsome, competent, good looking, smart, yes and a feminist because he respects women I'm sure, I can tell about these things. Where was I?"

Leaning back against a stack of pillows on her hospital bed, the corded hospital phone propped between her ear and her shoulder, Sabine inserted the last toe separator on her left foot in preparation for painting her toenails.

"Here, this one." Juliet handed her a bottle of Zoya non-animal tested nail polish in bright mauve, then turned her chair back to the makeshift desk that was the foot of Sabine's bed, and continued reading George Gallup's ***Adventures in Immortality*** from the Kindle app on her laptop. Through the tinny Kindle speakers streamed the theme from *A Man and a Woman* on Juliet's new station, Radio Pink Panther.

"Damn," Sabine said. "I can't believe all these years have gone by and the one time I'm not there, the handsome competent feminist scanner voice shows up in person at Telecomm. Who else saw him besides you?"

"Aja was here. She reminded me that he was younger than my grandson."

"Oh nonsense. She just wanted him for herself."

"Duh."

Sabine sighed. She was alright with the new intel that the handsome human behind the scanner voice was unattainable. Ultimately it was the acquiring of the information that was important. It didn't really matter what the content was. You just had to amass data, she forgot exactly why. "Gotta go. Yanina's here to figure out how I'm going to pay for all this, since my hospital employee insurance package doesn't cover anything."

"Don't get me started," said Glo. *"Hey, note to yourself. Tune your phone into the scanner's website, hello, right? You can listen to Handsome Voice and keep up with intel gathering at the same time."*

Sabine clicked the Safari button on her phone and entered the police scanner's website. There he was, the very handsome voice that she had missed because of her surgery. *"Cardiac situation, Echo Level, 42 Main Street. Male unresponsive after inserting scissors into wall outlet. CPR in progress."* And a few minutes later, *"Respiratory inhalation issue, Delta level, 68 Center Street. Unconscious person trying to fix furnace in attic."*

"He sounds handsome," said Juliet, looking up from Sabine's pinky toe.

"Doesn't he though?"

Yanina never wore much eye makeup, but what little eyeliner and mascara she wore had wound its way into the maze of creases under each eye, creating dripping black horizontal stripes that finally pooled into each eye bag. Her hair had been blond since it turned grey 20 years ago, and what little hair was left was charred from daily blow drying. "It's all stress-related," she had explained to Sabine and Glo years ago, "because my dermatologist prescribed Rogaine and it wasn't covered."

"I don't know how many nights I can authorize for Sabine to stay in the hospital," Yanina whispered to Juliet. "Her insurance for bullet holes covers one night. This makes me question my function as a child of God. I went into healthcare thinking I could, yes, well I'm just going to say it: help people."

"Don't question your calling, Yunky," Juliet whispered back. "We are merely pawns here on earth. Or do I mean peons? Anyway, Yunky, we're as innocent as ants. No one knows what's really going on or who is to blame."

Yanina's eyes widened and she shot a look at Juliet as if Juliet had just decoded the ICD-10 medical coding enigma. She whispered, "I mean, yes, I have no idea what's going on here. Why does that make me feel better?"

Sabine closed her eyes for a second, and found herself watching a generic noir art film from the '60s. A woman and a man in silhouette were standing in a dark street with hazy smoke lifting off the pavement. Sabine was watching the film from a white gazebo, sitting at a little wicker table, curling her hand around the stem of a crisp, sweating glass filled to the brim with Pinot Grigio. The sky was a pristine blue. The light was golden. A tiny, warm breeze gently teased the hem of her gossamer maxi-gown, revealing her smooth crossed legs and four-inch gold stilettos.

At the very same time, however, she was sitting on the bathroom floor at her mother's house in 1978, her back against the closed, locked door. Through the door she could hear her mother yelling incoherently at the television news about the Jim Jones murders in Guyana. Sabine was relieved to have a red plastic cup filled to the brim with a red dinner table blend, as she became lost in David Lynch's *Eraserhead*, which was being projected onto the opposite wall above the towel rack.

Sabine used her willpower to direct her consciousness away from *Eraserhead* and back to the warm, white gazebo. She stayed quiet because she wasn't quite sure what was going on. She knew from working at Trauma Town Dispatch that you needed to lay back until you learned the culture, the mythology, of your workplace. For instance: Who are the gods? Is lunch important? Can you hum the opening theme of *StarTrek Next Gen*?

More importantly, what did Grandmother Indigo mean when she said she had something important to share? Should Sabine go back to see what it is? Or should she continue travelling back to her body on earth to prolong the dimly-lit passage through the spongey denseness?

No matter. Sabine knew she didn't need to totally understand everything. She had seen enough *Twilight Zone* to know that whatever you think it is, that's not it.

Sabine opened her eyes and returned to her hospital bed. Juliet was screwing the cap back on the nail polish, and Sabine realized she had only been gone for a few seconds. As the room came into focus, she heard Juliet and Yunky discussing how the eleven dimensions are all interwoven and our brains are meager enough that we can only perceive one at a time. Thus sometimes different worlds blurred together.

"So yeah, I mean right? I could be in a different dimension right now and I'd think it was the normal earth dimension," Yunky said.

"That's a stunning observation, Yunky," Juliet said. "You should join Sabine and I next time we go to the Black Cat for drinks."

"So…Juliet. Um, yeah, I saw Tristan," Sabine said casually, as if she had bumped into him at the supermarket.

"Yes," Juliet said, just as casually. "He told me he saw you."

e86755etttt

Yunky finally collapsed into the one chair in Sabine's hospital room, and was starting to fall into a deep, noisy sleep. Her planner had fallen on the floor with the binder rings open, and notebook paper was scattered like leaves. Her phone, though, was still clutched tightly in her right hand.

"Tristan's very handsome," Sabine said, using her overly-neutral overhead announcement voice.

"Oh yes, and he just keeps getting better looking as he gets older."

"Ah. Which brings me to a question, Juliet."

"Oh for Godsake, I know. I get it. I'm clinging and it's driving him nuts."

"No, not that. Where on earth is Tristan from? I love his accent."

Juliet laughed and lifted her heavy tote off the floor and plopped it down on the foot of the bed. She was glowing. "I have the answer to all issues," she whispered.

Unzipping the top of the tote, she reached in and pulled out four small makeup bags she had received as free gifts from the Chanel counter at Saks Fifth Avenue when she lived some sort of Saks-based life in New York at some unknown point in her past. "Hospital food is not healthy, my dear. I brought something more life-enhancing."

"You know what Tristan said? What he wants to do?"

"Sabine. I've been married to the man for many many years. You have known him for a hundredth of a nanosecond."

"Of course, Juliet, you're absolutely right."

Juliet carefully lined up the four makeup bags. With the confident anticipatory smile of a magician, she slowly unzipped each bag and pulled out 8-ounce bottles of what appeared to be Welch's Grape Juice. She held up one of the bottles and looked at Sabine with a deep smile of knowing peace. It was Firehouse Merlot. Four servings.

It reminded Sabine of the time 15 years ago when she first moved to Trummel and the doctor said she was too nervous and prescribed her 100-count of 10-mg Valium with unlimited refills. Sabine remembered sinking deep into relief-mode and thinking, I'm set for life.

"I didn't mean to pry about Tristan," said Sabine. "I get it, I really do."

"Oh my dear, I didn't mean to make you feel bad," said Juliet. "Tristan was a player. He was his own man, not a family man."

"Is he close to your daughter in Budapest?"

"Oh yes, yes, he's fine. Linette is fine. We're all the three of us, really fine, except that he's dead."

"You are my hero, Juliet," said Sabine.

"You are my connection to the planet earth," said Juliet.

They clinked juice bottles. "To what shall we toast?" said Sabine.

"I love that question," Juliet answered. "Let's toast to Marianne Williamson's 'resonant field of disruptive miraculous possibilities'."

The women took thoughtful sips from their grape juice bottles.

"God, that's good," said Sabine. "You can't imagine all this time without Merlot, except of course all the nice wine I had on the other side."

"Ah yes," said Juliet softly as if remembering a hazy soft encounter of her own. "You need to know. Tristan was the allure of an unattainable man. He chose me, but then he left."

"Well I mean he didn't leave of his own accord, Juliet, he had cancer, right? I saw him on the other side."

"He left. Call it cancer, he still left. But I'm good, I'm okay, I get it. I think."

Sabine took a number of sips from her juice bottle. "I'm so sorry, dear neighbor, my friend. I wish I could help."

"You did help, Sabine. The fact that you saw him on the other side confirms the fact that yes, he's still … he's still … anyway, that I'm not completely nuts. right?"

"If you're nuts, we're both nuts."

"It opens the portal to infinite fields of energy and information. By the way, Nyx has some deep intel she wanted me to give to you. That file they have on you?"

"Yeah?"

"Nyx said the algorhythm pointed to an Inquiry."

"I've just had brain surgery."

"Nyx said you might be in serious trouble with Henry Moho and the commanders at Human Resources."

"Of course, but there's someone else I met."

"Who?"

"Your third great grandmother?"

"You found Great great great Grandmother Indigo? I've been looking for her, there hasn't been a trace of what happened to her."

"She talked about tardigrades."

"Oh how funny, Sabine. She always had a thing for tardigrades."

Chapter 13

Two things Sabine never got over: Dr. Strangelove and Bambi.
Two things Juliet was still processing: Tristan's quantum entanglement and Fellini's 8 ½ .

Sabine leaned over her bathroom sink to get closer to the mirror. It was the first time since she had been shot that she was able to get her black eyeliner on her actual eyes, as opposed to the various black and blue swellings and green bruises. She was starting to look normal again.

Freddie Mercury, his orange fur coated with a light dusting of Bobbi Brown translucent face powder, was napping in the sink. Higgs-Boson was in the still wet tub, lapping up the remaining drops of water by the drain, and Dr. Crusher was trying to fit into a Q-tip box on the counter. Peace. Same-dom. Quiet. Home.

Sabine had been using the same black eyeliner since junior high school in the late sixties. She liked her eyes to be heavy with makeup, even though now the powders fell into the little wrinkles. Eye makeup to Sabine was like wearing glasses - over the years she developed the personal mythology that she couldn't see without her eye makeup on. Who's to say it didn't work - she never did have to wear actual glasses.

The wrinkles were easy to ignore, since Plastics was just two floors above Telecomm and running up there to get Botox - should, say, it be required if the owner of one of the handsome dismembered voices from the police scanner ever materialized and was age appropriate. Yes, Glo claimed to have seen a realized version of one of those things, but it was just "odd" that no one else saw him except Aja.

Ultimately, though, Sabine didn't make the wrinkle thing real because she knew that enormous changes lurked just beneath the blink of that eye, and could leap out and surprise her with no warning. One day you're walking down the street thinking about donuts and the next instant there you are, waking up in the ER missing, say, an ear. Sabine ultimately didn't care that black eyeliner over wrinkles when you're 64 was different than, say, sunscreen and lip gloss when you were 20. She knew from hanging around Juliet and also from her meeting with Juliet's third great-grandmother that her body was a transient convenience allowing her to access stuff she couldn't access as the non-corporeal entity that she often believed she actually was. Indeed, Sabine now realized, the time spent hauling the physical body around the planet had to be used cleverly because it went by in a flash. The seventies were a moment before, the next century a nanosecond to come.

Sabine finished her makeup and pulled on a thick, soft, pale pink sweater and black silk pants. She combed her silky brown hair and spritzed hairspray on her bangs to keep them straight. As the cat swarm watched, she put on a pair of small gold hoop earrings and her black high-heeled boots. Living in the middle of nowhere didn't mean she had to dress like it. Juliet was proof of that.

A light knocking on the door sent Dr. Crusher running for cover under the bed. Sabine's stomach fluttered in repressed panic as it always did when there was an intruder alert such as a doorbell, a ringing phone, or an intruding thought from the Trauma Town experience. To alleviate her phone and text tone startle response, she had tried different ring tones over the years - Tibetan bells, seagulls over a soft ocean surf - to deactivate her panic reflex, but nothing worked, so she reached outward toward the drama as she had learned to do.

At Trauma Town, drama was life. Perched at her operator's station waiting for the code phone to go off, or strobe lights to suddenly start swirling around, or an ER patient to swallow a thermometer and have to be flown to Mass General, gave Sabine the skill to focus her entire awareness on calm centering, even while waiting for an immanent pan-explosion.

Sabine opened her door. Her system calmed immediately and she smiled with relief as she saw Juliet. "Oh, okay. I'm fine, I'm fine."

Juliet was in her gold satin lingerie, full maquillage, and bare feet. "You were screaming in your sleep last night, sweetie. It was so loud I heard it through the wall." A shaft of early evening golden sun from Sabine's sliding door in the living room illuminated Juliet's loose, golden hair. In Juliet's hand, like an afterthought, was a tulip glass filled with champagne.

"Yes of course. Come in, I'm getting ready for work. Tell me what shoes to wear."

Juliet floated gently in, and the two women went into Sabine's walk-in closet. Sabine's life had just shifted from raw panic with the cats running for cover, to sublime perfumed softness. Dr. Crusher joined them in the closet and the three of them sat on the plush carpeted floor and stared at a row of Sabine's shoes.

"Ah! Here we go." Juliet held up a pair of black patent leather four-inch stilettos with ankle ties. "These would be perfect for the hospital switchboard."

Dr. Crusher rubbed up against Juliet, who put the shoes down and stroked the tiny gray creature.

"Those," said Sabine. "I kind of was saving them for a date night."

"Oh of course." Juliet put the shoes back. "Sorry."

"I was screaming in my sleep again? What was I saying?"

"Something about Jack and Jill bathrooms."

"Damn. I thought I was over that."

"Tristan says that my grandmother Indigo gave you the key to deciphering the files."

"Um… hmmm… I hope I didn't forget… I don't remember that." Sabine, realizing that no one would see her anyway, unless the hospital oxygen cut-off snapped again and the fire department had to rush in to prevent the place from a catastrophic explosion, slipped on the black patent leather four-inch stilettos and secured the Velcro ankle ties. "Except that I have the feeling it's something. Something obvious."

Juliet stretched her legs out in front of her on the carpet and leaned back against the built-in dresser, arranging her gold satin robe so it covered her knees. "What we think of as linear time, my dear Sabine, don't forget - it's all a ruse." She took a sip of her champagne and then passed the glass to Sabine, who was sitting cross-legged under a pastel swirl of scarves and belts.

Freddie Mercury tip-toed in, began a loud purring fit, and stepped with entitlement onto Juliet's lap. "Alright, little mister, at least I get to go home after this. Sabine has to live with you."

Higgs-Boson poked her small white and gray head in as she kept watch just outside the closet door.

Sabine sipped the champagne and felt it land in a bubbling pit of bile in the bottom of her stomach as she remembered why she was screaming in her sleep. Tristan had told her he wanted to move on but was unable to because he couldn't leave Juliet alone. It felt to Sabine that he had confessed to cheating. She felt betrayed for Juliet. She felt betrayed for herself. If Juliet couldn't trust her dead husband, then how could anyone ever trust anything?

"Aortic valve burst" said the handsome scanner voice. Naming the name in an even tone, knowing what was going on, his voice made Sabine feel safe. She relaxed a little as she acknowledged her earthly life.

Sabine was back at Telecomm with the handsome scanner voice – an authority entity that was neutral with just the hint of the learned decision to not judge anything. That choice for kindness made the voice very attractive, gave him a uniform, turned him into a hero, someone who would come and save you if anything were to happen. Not like Tristan.

Sabine was alone in the twilight cave. Glo was on break and Aja hadn't come in yet. Aside from some really bad headaches and a tickling in her left ear that made her think there was something crawling in there, she had recovered well from Clea shooting her in the head.

"Aortic valve burst from possible electrocution. Fourteen Main Street at The Accordion Connection. Echo level."

Ah - that must be Jeanette. She had been in the conference room, lost, on the other side. Sabine flashed briefly on her own discomfort with Jeanette's departure being out of sequence, and then relaxed into the familiar ungraspable.

"Trummel Hospital, can you hold please? Thank you."

Line 2: "Trummel Hospital, can you hold? Thank you."

Line 3: "Hospital, hold please."

Line 4: "Hold."

Line 5: "Hold on I'm coming."

Line 1: "Thank you for holding, how may I direct your call?"

The operators used to answer with "How can I help you?" but that quickly turned into a soft landing field for Trummel's lost. *"Oh thank God I'm speaking to an actual person. I haven't had anything to eat in four days,"* one caller said. "Can you make it to the emergency room?" Sabine responded. *"No. I'm having a diabetic emergency and my grandson is in college in Omaha."* "Okay, then, can you hang up and call 911?" *"No, I have electromagnetic hypersensitivity."* "Yes of course. Hold on, I'm going to connect you with 911, okay?" *"Bless you, child."* "Don't hang up."

Walking up two flights of stairs from Telecomm to the main level in her 4-inch stiletto heels, and then up another four flights to the admin level - instead of taking the elevator - was actually quite clever, Sabine thought, because now she wouldn't have to do any calisthenics when she got home.

The band o' cats loved calisthenics because Sabine was on the floor with them, doing amusing things. Higgs-Boson liked to hover over her face and purr loudly. Freddie Mercury sat on her stomach, possibly imitating goat-yoga-consciousness. Dr. Crusher searched first for a ray of sunlight to bask in, and often finding just the closed curtains, retreated to under the bed to clean her toes.

Glo had finally arrived in the switchboard room with the news that Human Resources had called and Sabine was to go up to the fourth floor for a quick meeting. "They have computer programs that can decode things," Glo complained. "My grandson Izzy has a decoder ring. I can't believe HR is still stuck on deciphering those paper files. No wonder the hospital is losing money."

"Maybe it's some sort of personality test," Sabine mused. "Maybe someone from the PUF is conducting research into behavioral traits in humans challenged with confusion."

"Oh good, the Psych Unit's in on it," Glo said. Then into her headset: "Trummel Hospital, can you hold please? No, not you, I'm sure you don't need the Psych Unit, my deepest apologies. Hold for Telemetry." Then back to Sabine. "I met Nyx in the deli bar of the cafeteria, she was cleaning up from a shaved nose incident with the cheese slicer. Lots of blood. She said she saw the file they have on you and for you to watch your step."

Sabine got to the fourth floor, a little winded but feeling pretty good except that her feet hurt. Note to self, buy only round-toed stilettos from now on to leave room for toe expansion. Her mind wandered through cyberspace searching for the possibility of finding round-toed stilettos, and then thinking perhaps she should buy cat litter through Chewy.com instead of lugging it home from the supermarket, and finally sorting through how it might feel to be going about your day, slicing some cheese for a sandwich, only to find that your life was turned suddenly upside down because you accidentally sliced off part of your nose.

She walked down the carpeted fourth floor hallway toward HR, wondering how much pain one might experience from a sliced nose and coming to the conclusion that probably not that much because you'd go into shock. So it would be okay. Shock was a protection mechanism.

"Sabine. Come in." Sherri's door was open. She was sitting behind a large metal desk piled with paper, print-outs, notebooks, a framed picture of a small child, and a mug with a greyed-out square that said *Your Photo Here*. "Please. Have a seat."

"Oh, thank you," Sabine said with exaggerated politeness. Ever since her last ex from Brooklyn lost their entire retirement account by investing it in a small start-up that was designing a giant magnet to shield the earth from incoming asteroids, she knew she probably shouldn't lose her job. Yes, she had loved her ex at the time, but lately she was wondering how far she might go for love the next time if she hadn't already lost everything. That was seventeen years ago and she was still trying to rebuild some sort of savings just in case something happened and she couldn't make it to the supermarket for more Firehouse Merlot.

"Sabine Covina," Sherri said, looking up from her papers.

"Why, yes," Sabine said. "Is everything okay?"

"Our work here in HR is to facilitate the exchange of mutual co-conveniences in order to affect real yet transcendent outcomes that benefit the community as well as the team members of the ...." she paused, out of breath. Dark bags appeared under eyes as if from nowhere.

"You guys up here are amazing that way," Sabine said.

"Yes, well, we're concerned about the QA Cloud."

"Oh yes. Me too."

"I'm glad you understand. We hired a consulting firm to facilitate our Quality Assurance Cloud, and we received a report that there has been an inordinate amount of F-7 entries into the cloud from your computer."

"Oh yes, I utilize F-7 frequently."

"Well, there is the issue of an overuse of the F7 function key," Sherri said gingerly. "Perhaps even a compulsive F7 obsession."

Sabine loved F7, it allowed for her data entry in reports to be accurate. "F7 erases stuff," she explained, as if she were saying the sun makes the flowers grow.

228 / Suzann Kale

"Yes, precisely." Sherri leaned forward across her desk. "That's the problem. You can't just F-7 everything. There needs to be a paper trail."

"Paper, yes of course. I love paper."

"Someone tried to F-7 the Incident Report involving your elevator encounter with the unfortunate Denize Leclair."

"Oh. That's ... awful."

"You know I'm never comfortable in these situations, Sabine. But it seems there was the issue with the actual elevator encounter itself, over and above F-7ing the report."

"Yes. Well I would have no idea who would try to delete the report. And Denize Leclair was already there in the elevator when I got on. She was in her nightgown with blood everywhere. I tried to keep her from falling."

"You're second tier, Sabine. You are not supposed to have direct contact with patients, except through the switchboard."

"I know but -"

"Should something happen, we wouldn't be covered."

"- but she was falling."

"She still fell."

"Maybe not as bad as if I hadn't been there to try to catch her."

"And you fell, too."

"Yes because Denize fell on top of me."

Sherri leaned back in her chair, closed her eyes, and did an exaggerated deep breathing routine. It made Sabine flash on her late mother the victim who used to exit a difficult situation by retreating into dramatic pseudo-empathic fainting episodes. Sherri opened her eyes, smiled, and leaned forward. "The thing is, Sabine. There are HIPAA repercussions."

"Oh dear."

"Yes."

"Oh my."

"Yes. Security reports that the Duress Alarm went off just before you got into the elevator."

A light lit, and Sabine suddenly smiled as if this new piece of information just solved the problem. She took a deep breath of relief. "Oh, okay. Not a problem, Sherri," she said. "That was a coincidence. One had nothing to do with the other."

"Sabine, the alarm was for a Code Yellow - a missing patient! Nurse Tzofia couldn't find Denize and pushed the Duress alarm."

"So yes, Sherri, there it is in plain sight. It wasn't my mistake. The Duress alarm is for Code Grays."

"Well she pushed it with a Code Yellow situation."

"But a Code Gray signals a combative patient or menacing visitors with like guns."

"Sabine, there was a missing patient! Okay, that's all I have. Your file will reflect that you misinterpreted a Code Gray for a Code Yellow. Or - well a Code Yellow for a Code Gray. You can't misinterpret codes, people's lives depend on it. And if the Duress Alarm went off, why did you feel it necessary to run out physically to the elevator?"

"Oh! No, no, I was already in the elevator."

"Well that's not the protocol, Sabine."

The Duress Alarm was an electronic device that had been built into the wall in Telecomm behind the engineer's desk in the back that no one ever sat at. From there it had apparently been wired into different hospital departments, seemingly at random. No one knew exactly what to do with it. You could press a button from, say, PUF, the psych unit, if someone were being combative, and it would sound in the switchboard room in Telecomm, but no one knew what happens after that, and no one who pushed their buttons in PUF knew what to expect as a response.

Three months before, Mr. Ng had fallen out of bed and smashed his head against his wife's CPAP machine which she had left on the floor, and lost consciousness. Nurse Tzofia pushed this button but then wasn't sure if it went anywhere, so she also called a code into Telecomm. Sabine took the code information from Tzofia, all the while the Duress Alarm was shrieking, but the digital panel was announcing a Code Blue. Apparently the software was routed in such a way that if the Duress Alarm signaled a Code Blue, that meant it was actually a Code Gray. Everyone knew that, it was a given.

Sabine summarized this Incident. "It is what it is, then." She smiled. It wasn't Sherri's fault, there must have been some mix-up in the Office of the Grand Weaver, as Juliet might say. Thank heaven for Juliet who was able to keep sanity close by during periods of earthly unravelings.

Sabine felt another stab of anger again at Tristan for leaving Juliet, then she felt gratitude that despite his own needs, Tristan was still staying close by to watch over Juliet. Then Sabine was furious that he wanted to leave Juliet to go into the Light or wherever - then she felt panic that if anything broke in her condo and they had to get in to fix it that the cats might get out and get lost. This prompted a vision of Freddie, Higgs, and Dr. Crusher wandering around the streets in the cold, hungry and frightened. Someone might pick them up and take them to a medical lab. They could be run over by a teenager. They could be separated.

"Sabine, are you alright?" Sherri actually sounded concerned. "Sabine?"

Tears were streaking mascara down Sabine's cheeks and creating white stripes where her three coats of mineral powder and blush had been. "Why yes, yes, I'm fine Sherri. Thank you." She grabbed the last Kleenex from the box on Sherri's desk. "Is that it?"

"Yes of course, dear." Sherri was younger than Sabine and should not be playing the "dear" card. Only older people can call younger people "dear." But no matter, Sabine thought, Sherri is in a very difficult position and probably hates her job.

Sabine felt she had to comfort the poor girl. "It will all be okay, you know."

Sherri was caught off-guard and her face went blank. A second later the life came back and she said, "Sabine, there is this other document in your file, I don't know if you were aware of it."

"What?"

"The PUF has diagnosed you with ODD - oppositional defiance disorder."

"That's actually quite odd," Sabine said. "I've never been to the Psych Unit."

Sabine quickly searched the RAM files in her head, and landed on the night two years ago when the night nurse couldn't figure out how to unforward her calls from going to the morgue. That would have been

Sabine's only personal contact with the PUF. But then Sabine remembered Nyx saying something about the transcriptionist who had been having rage blackouts because her fiancée had just been diagnosed with PACS - Post Ashram Composting Syndrome - for hoarding eggshells and avocado pits. So instead of typing in his actual diagnosis of AHS, Alien Hand Syndrome, which is when your hand slaps you in the face every time you go for the peanut butter, the transcriptionist typed in ODD, oppositional defiance disorder. And she typed it in a file marked Sabine Covina, Nyx said, because someone had to be blamed and Sabine's file had been opened in order to give her the one-time clearance to get into the PUF to fix the phone which had been mistakenly forwarded to the morgue.

A couple's muted discussion bled through Sherri's door from the hall. "Damn it, Alison, the next thing you know they tell you I'm sorry we gotta pull your lung out." "Yes, dear, the whole thing is just awful."

"Sabine," Sherri said. Her face was suddenly sagging, and Sabine thought she looked frightened. "I'm afraid we're going to have to let you go."

Chapter 14

Sabine's youth was informed by Handel's Messiah and also the Grateful Dead's Truckin'. Juliet's grandmother, a lyric soprano, sang Que Sera Sera in the limo every time they went to City Island for Sunday dinner. Juliet had trouble ever since, getting that song loop out of her head.

The good thing about crises was that you could sit in bed indefinitely with your cluster of cats, and drink Merlot. If you added your life's Pandora background music from your Laurie Anderson *Strange Angels* station, why there you were, being proactive - staying a nanosecond ahead of point-of-no-return panic. Sometimes being in crisis felt cozy and sheltered.

"Juliet."

"Hello?"

"It's Sabine. I'm drunk dialing."

"You must be running low then - I'll bring over some more Firehouse."

"Door's open."

Some things just stick - like Sabine having to use see-through shower curtains all her life, even though ***Psycho*** came out in 1960.

"I've been studying life as dream," Juliet said as she kicked off her feather-topped high-heeled sandals and squeezed onto the man side of Sabine's bed, between Freddie and Higgs-Boson. Dr. Crusher always slept at the bottom, away from confrontation. Freddie meowed crankily and Higgs jumped off and headed for the sandbox. "So I brought champagne." She handed Sabine a flute glass and poured from her half-empty bottle of Moët & Chandon. "This was Tristan's and my wedding champagne."

As Sabine savored the cold, bitter liquid, and felt its bubbles spray through her nervous system, she realized the potential of everything possibly being okay. "This was your wedding champagne? Why didn't you drink it at the wedding?"

"No, it was our champagne," Juliet said. "Like some people have their song."

"Oh."

"Tristan and I celebrated life as dream. That was our thing. And now that he's molecularly compromised, I have to drink by myself."

"I imagine he can't keep anything down at this point, let alone champagne."

"He told me that he upset you by saying he wanted to move on."

"I just thought that was rather abrupt of him. A husband is supposed to be there for you. Not run off somewhere into some light."

Juliet sipped her champagne. "I found a new anti-aging cream at the Walmart," she said. "I'm going to try it tonight, see what happens."

"Juliet, what will you do if he leaves you?"

"For heaven's sake, Sabine. I'll join a gym and get a new wardrobe."

"No really."

"I don't know. Look for him elsewhere, I suppose. Although I don't want to be clingy."

"They hate me at the hospital."

"Of course they don't. I've been there with you. They adore you."

"Where will you look for him? I mean, I saw lots of nooks and hidden rooms and alternate hallways when I was on the other side. Alleys and little neighborhoods, underground bars. Tristan could be anywhere."

Juliet paused. "You saw Grandmother Indigo."

"Yes. Yes I did." It was a secret that only she and Juliet shared. Grandmother Indigo had the key to Henry Moho's files.

Juliet laughed slightly, took a deep breath, and reached for an available cat to hold. Dr. Crusher was the only one left on the bed, and he jumped off as he saw Juliet's red nails and bracelets come toward him.

Sabine awoke with a start and grabbed her phone. It said 3:37am. Juliet had fallen asleep on the man side of the bed, her empty champagne flute on its side. Freddie Mercury had come back to bed and was curled up happily on Juliet's left arm.

Sabine felt an aura of panic, because Things were out of place. "Call Trauma Town Dispatch," she whispered to Siri.

"*Thank you for calling Trummel Hospital, how may I direct your call?*" It was Glo, Heavens be blessed.

"Glo it's me."

"*Oh my freaking God, Sabine.*"

"I know."

"*They didn't fire you, you have to know that.*"

"I know, Glo. We are a hospital family."

"*Just remember that, okay?*"

"Of course."

"*They simply escorted you off the premises oh and with no more paychecks.*"

"Yes. Life in the TraumaVerse."

"*Absolutely. You'll be back in no time. As long as you can give Henry Moho what he wants.*"

"Okay." Sabine knew Glo was right. They were a sisterhood, the Sisterhood of the Switchboard, the Darlings of Dispatch even if in their own minds.

Sitting in the windowless depths of the hospital interior, capped with headsets, Sabine, Glo, and Aja - and daytime operators Valentine, Teshuna, and Wing - kept watch over communications. They shared everything - surgeons' backlines, daily morgue lists, ambulance drivers' handsomeness ratings.

And then there was the time when Tom from Plant had subcontracted a crew to fix the vents on the hospital roof and they cut the oxygen lines by mistake, creating a Code White. Code Whites are situations that have the potential to turn into MCI's, mass casualty incidents. So not only was there no oxygen in Telemetry for the heart and lung patients to breathe - but leaking oxygen, being highly flammable, meant that the hospital and all surrounding buildings could suddenly explode.

Sabine remembered that particular Code White fondly. It was the time she and Glo, both new to the hospital, made the conscious decision to go down with the ship. There was no way they weren't going to stay at their stations, set up the Command Center, get the fire department there, keep urgent information flowing, and coordinate movements between Admin, Plant, Security, Fire, and all the floor the nurses.

Sabine and Glo, both hyperventilating from the excitement, had locked eyes, smiled in recognition of neither knew what, and went back to their overhead warning announcements and inter-departmental instructions.

When Yanina, the utilization review nurse from down the hall, burst into the switchboard room, wild-eyed and sweating, and shouted "This place could blow at any second," Sabine and Glo knew that they were soul sisters forever.

In moments, though, the muscular Fire Department hero guys did arrive in time and took control of the broken oxygen line. There was no explosion to grab the next day's headlines. And after that, Sabine and Glo had an unspoken bond - the switchboard operators who could have been blown up but weren't. Glo sometimes complained of nightmares after that, but eventually the whole thing became legend.

But mostly the Telecomm switchboard operators shared the unspoken guilty high of needing to be part of the crises. The stomach-turning thrill of the code phone suddenly howling. The arrythmiatic wait for the next catastrophe to happen. The race to the microphone to overhead page a helicopter, or a car with its headlights left on, or anything with "stat" after it.

Sabine knew she was in the middle of nowhere, but she felt gratitude that she was in the middle. The middle meant yes, aha, you were not actually nowhere because the middle was the heart of it all.

"But you must decipher Henry's files," Glo said, lurching Sabine back to the present. *"That's all I can think of that will save us. He's minutes away from installing an automated phone answering system which is sure to drive people mad - well, more mad than they already are."*

"I'm on the very brink of deciphering the files, Glo. Juliet's third great grandmother is helping me."

"Okay, good, whatever. Just do it fast.. Every tiny piece of intel is useful. Each little nano-threadlette of subatomic mini-knowledge has value. I'm using Juliet-speak here, so you'll understand me."

"Yes, I get it, Glo, for Godsake."

"Before the end of the world kicks in. I have no savings and second ex-husband lost our retirement investing in Pimpjuice. As that started to go under, he salvaged some remains and invested in a phone book company. Like paper phone books."

In the background, Sabine heard her handsome hero voice on the Telecomm police scanner, like he was a lost lover. *"Woman fallen in tub two days ago, has been there ever since."* It made her remember her mission in life as a ... whatever it was that Juliet was, and she felt a temporary sense of blessed false calm.

"Just saying," Glo was still talking. *"In my life? No more guys with beards who drink beer in jeans. Any new man in my life better be a neurosurgeon or I'm over it. Oh, just an FYI Sabine."*

"Yes?"

"I heard through Nyx that Trummel Hospital is going under."

"Going under? What does that mean? Has there been a broken water main?"

"No, I wish. Apparently we've run out of money."

"The hospital ran out of money?"

"Near-functioning pathogenically challenged hysterical person. Seventy-two Main Street, ground floor. Bravo Level oh eight-hundred." The confident, even-toned masculine we're-all-over-it police scanner voice, as always, soothed Sabine's nerves. She took a deep breath, released the tension in her neck, and felt her heartbeat slow down to normal.

Next to Sabine, Juliet opened her eyes and, at the sight of Freddie Mercury on her left arm, screamed in shock. Freddie's ears went back and he dove off the bed to undisclosed places where cats go in condos where no one can find them. Juliet sat up, pulled her champagne flute to her chest, and looked around the room as if she had suddenly found herself on one of Neptune's moons.

"Gotta go, Glo," Sabine whispered, and clicked off her phone.

"Alright, Sabine. This is it," said Raphael. "We need to see if there's anything in these files that will help you, we need some food and drink, and where is our life's background music?"

Sabine had dragged herself next door to Juliet's condo in order to give the cats a chance to regroup. She had offered Raphael an exclusive, although neither of them knew to what. Juliet had gone out for a walk to look for front porches with their lights left on during the day, in order to forestall what she said was an incoming melancholia. Sabine had not changed out of the yoga pants and pink hoodie with *Trauma Town* written on the front, that she had been wearing since she took to her bed with her Merlot the day before.

Raphael's curly dark hair was a bit overgrown, and he hadn't shaved in perhaps three days. That, with his jeans and dark plaid felt shirt and the few pounds he had recently gained made him look almost huggable.

"Here's your exclusive backstory, Raphael," Sabine said. "They've apparently realized there is a switchboard room with human telephone operators in it." Sabine spread out the file folders and their contents onto the glass coffee table as she had done many times over the last few months. "They are onto us, as I had feared, and word is IT is in the process of installing an automated telephone tree."

Raphael sat on the floor next to Sabine. He looked her in the eye. "I am the messenger. I take my job seriously. The people of Trummel need to know this. Why was Juliet in such a hurry to go for her walk?"

"My cat Freddie slept on her arm last night."

Raphael got up with a groan as if there was a musculoskeletal pain starting up somewhere, went to Juliet's entertainment corner, and put on *The Monkey's Paw* from Laurie Anderson's *Strange Angels*. *"The gift of life it's a shot in the dark; It's the call of the wild; It's the big wheel, The big ride…"*

"Raphael."

He came back to the glass coffee table and sank again into the deep beige carpet. "Sabine."

"I'm serious. Look at this." A small dark object had fallen from file number 3 onto the glass coffee table.

"Jesus, Sabine. It's a bug. I hate bugs."

"I hate bugs too." She scooted back.

"So we found an insect. I can't run that on page one."

The front door opened and Juliet, stunning in a creamy white fleece sweat suit, fresh-faced and

244 / Suzann Kale

invigorated from the cold, stood by the oversized mirror in the front hall and slipped off her gold colored sneakers.

"Did you find the porch lights?" Sabine called to her.

"Yes, there were enough porch lights so I'm realizing there's something else going on."

"Oh. Okay, well, this may help. We're on the verge of the final decryption," Sabine said, now in a softer voice as Juliet came into the livingroom and joined Sabine and Raphael on the floor.

"I tried to float above my body to get above the battlefield, so to speak," Juliet said. "It didn't work. Maybe I need to lose some weight. Oddly, though, the porch lights just made me feel worse. So I thought maybe if I looked into people's windows, that might help. Seeing people living their lives."

"Uh oh," Raphael said, not looking up from the files.

"No, no, everything's fine," Juliet said. "It's just that I had this urge to go into strangers' homes and sit in their livingrooms. I didn't of course, but that's all I could think about."

"Strangers' livingrooms?" Sabine tried to sound nonchalant.

"Yes. Strangers. Like, someplace warm, where I could … you know Tristan wants to leave me."

Raphael looked up from the files on the table.

"Juliet," Sabine whispered. "Tristan is ... how can I say this. He's ..."

"He's dead," Raphael said, and then looked down again as if realizing he had almost just yelled.

"Oh I know all that." Juliet took a deep breath, as if deciding it was time to confide in her friends. "But Tristan's been living here with me ever since. And now he wants to move on."

Sabine's delicate sense of balance was shaken by Juliet's distress. She felt she had to say something helpful, but all that came out was, "It's all fluid, you know."

"Yes but how will I find him? And what if he's, like, tired of me?" Juliet got up and went over to the entertainment center. "I think I've been a bit needy. If I were him I'd go to some other frequency too." Her voice was even and clear, non-emotional, almost android-like.

As the soft recessed lights enveloped Juliet in a golden glow, Sabine felt reassured about her friend's goddessness. Juliet was a total non-victim. Perhaps a saint, albeit a fragile one.

Juliet changed the station to *Radio Schizoid Chillout* playing *Whatever Happened to Gus*, as Sabine and Raphael looked on, empty of answers, no data to share.

"Okay," Sabine finally said. "Who is pouring, what are we drinking, and let's get in touch with that bastard Tristan."

Chapter 15

Sabine was shaped early on by the nightmare of knocking on strangers' doors trying to sell Girl Scout cookies.
Juliet was informed in fifth grade by Edith Hamilton's Mythology: Timeless Tales of Gods and Heroes.

Fifteen minutes of silence went by as Juliet and Raphael poured over the now mangled paper files on Juliet's glass coffee table which was now riddled with wet-wine-glass circles and fingerprints. Sabine sat cross-legged on the carpet under the entertainment center, trying to contact Tristan.

Finally Juliet broke the silence. "You don't have to find him, Sabine," she said gently. "I see him every day. I'll tell him."

Sabine opened her eyes, but kept her meditation pose. "What will you tell him, Juliet?"

"I'll tell him to move ahead into the light or wherever it is he wants to go. I'm fine, really."

And then Sabine and Juliet were sitting at a sidewalk café table at *Le Petit Prince de Paris* in a hidden corner of the Left Bank. The street lamps radiated a sparkly dusky gray in the slanted, early evening light. A crowd had gathered across the cobblestone court way at Shakespeare & Company for a lecture on *From Here to Eternity: Traveling the World to Find the Good Death* by Caitlin Doughty, but their voices were muted. Traffic was light, and through a gauze screen, they could still see Raphael in Juliet's livingroom, pouring over the files.

"I'm honestly terrified to leave you." Tristan was there at the café table. "I do love you, Juliet. It's just that you have no idea what awaits us on the other side. It makes earth look like a cardboard cut-out. An inconsequential dream. A flat picture with no raison d'être."

Raphael, unaware of any dimensional changes, continued to place papers thoughtfully next to other papers, as if they were puzzle pieces - studying some, placing others in different piles, starting a new pile on the floor next to him.

As the three watched Raphael through the gauze, he flipped through a small composition notebook from the top file, and suddenly fell backward.

"Wait, I've seen this before," said Sabine.

"Yes," said Tristan, "but this time we need to pay attention."

"Tristan, darling, are we micromanaging again?" said Juliet, in a higher voice that Sabine had not heard before. "Or - gosh." A slight, embarrassed laugh, and then her dark, inflectionless voice kicked back in.

"Sorry. Good God, I don't know where that came from. Perhaps random entities from the ether."

Something had fallen out of the notebook. A large insect. After a pause, Raphael laughed in relief - the insect was flattened, quite dead, and had been there for a while.

From the entertainment center, Laurie Anderson was singing *"Strange angels - singing just for me. Old stories - they're haunting me."*

"Alright, ladies, here we are," Tristan said.

Sabine thought he looked more ravaged than usual, with a five o'clock shadow made more pronounced by pale skin and stunning dark under eye circles.

"It's action time, dear wife and friend of dear wife," Tristan said. "Observe."

"I'm all over it," said Sabine. "Observe what?"

"Tristan, are we being obscure again?" Juliet sneezed, rummaged through her pearled handbag for a tissue, and added, "Yes, sorry, I don't know what came over me, it's evidently more than I can handle but I'm coping."

"Oh Juliet." Sabine felt she had to fix this if her world was ever going to make sense again. "You cope beautifully, you always do. Hold on, okay? Let's see

250 / Suzann Kale

how this plays out. Everything is going to be okay. I
promise."

"Yes of course." Juliet had her gold compact out
and was tapping away at mascara dings on her
cheekbones. "

"Here we go," said Tristan, aware of Juliet's
distress but moving ahead anyway. "Look - Raphael
opened a file and a dead bug fell out. He's about to
pick it up and throw it in the garbage. You both need to
get back there right away. This bug-like form is the
marker that Grandmother Indigo told Sabine to watch
for."

"Oh yes, of course!" Sabine said. "That's what
she said. I remember now."

"Well whatever, the poor man is sweating and
he looks unwell," Juliet said. "I've actually never seen
such frayed forehead furrow lines on such a young,
handsome man."

"Okay, but let's focus on our action items," said
Tristan. "You know I love you, Juliet, right? You and
me, it's you and me. Or it was. Always"

Juliet sipped her drink. Sabine noticed that it
was a generic drink, not the usual hyper-realistic deep
red velvet drink that she was accustomed to seeing on
the other side. Perhaps, Sabine decided, it was
because Juliet was focused on Tristan at that moment,
and nothing else mattered.

"I know, Tristan," Juliet whispered. Lipstick on the rim.

"You'll join me soon." Tristan's voice went low, as if for Juliet only. He paused to make sure he caught his wife's eye. "We will again be sipping Dom Pérignon on *Le Pont des Arts* overlooking the River Seine and the Louvre." He watched her to make sure she heard him. "You love Caravaggio's *The Fortune Teller*, remember? Yes?"

"Okay then." A tear slipped out of Juliet's left eye. Her compact was still in her hand, but she didn't bother to check her makeup for damage. "It's just that I'm a little tired, that's all."

As Tristan moved in to hold Juliet, he was suddenly gone - and Juliet and Sabine were back with Raphael on the floor around the coffee table, in Juliet's condo.

"Don't throw that out!" Sabine yelled to Raphael.

"What. It's a dead bug," said Raphael.

The squashed creature was on the coffeetable.

"It's a tardigrade," said Sabine.

Sabine, Juliet, and Raphael looked at the tardigrade.

"Although, hmm. Grandmother Indigo said you can't squash a tardigrade, so this couldn't be a squashed tardigrade," said Sabine. "So then what is it, if not a squashed tardigrade?"

"It's a USB flash drive," Juliet said.

Raphael, astonished, studied the bug. "Why yes, Juliet. Yes it certainly is."

"This is what Grandmother Indigo was telling us to look for," Sabine said. "This is it. It's what's in these files, what Henry Moho wanted us to find."

Juliet's EuroTechno Jazz Blues Internet radio station kicked in with their hit from 1984, *Très Fatigué*.

"So, yeah, I'm with you. So, what's a tardigrade?" Raphael was sweating. He pulled his gray cable knit cardigan off over his head amidst a flurry of static pops, and slapped it onto the couch. "It's hot in here. Juliet, for heavens sake how high do you keep the heat in this place?"

Chapter 16

Sabine's search for inner peace began at a young age with a cork screw. It transitioned to the ceremonial opening of Firehouse Merlot and the ritual pouring of the red velvet elixir into a vintage etched Tiffany wine glass.

Sabine's Tiffany wine glasses from her first wedding gift stash 42 years ago had long since been lost or broken, but she was always able to find delicately stemmed glasses at the various Walmarts throughout her life.

Sabine's cooking consciousness ended in fifth grade, watching her mother stuff animal flesh into a home meat grinder to make Shepherd's Pie. But she still was able, later in life, to create a concept fantasy of a warm and safe, happy kitchen.

It was a fantasy of being saturated in soothing amber evening light, with a gentle but capable handsome guy adding basil and tomato sauce to a pan of simmering onions and garlic, sipping his wine and recounting his day of saving children and dogs. Steam from a pot of boiling pasta filled the small love-filled space with a magical haze - oh and also there would have to be sleeping cats nearby and Chilldesiac smooth jazz streaming *Space Station Soma* from a high-end Bluetooth somewhere.

Sabine's dream, however, was threatened by the stark reality of *Star Trek*'s Beverly Crusher saying, "If there's nothing wrong with me, maybe there's something wrong with the universe." This was when the universe was disappearing around her. It made Sabine wonder about pre-destination.

Sabine thought back to her afterlife experience and realized that, although it had café tables with party lights, it had no cozy kitchen. And Tristan, handsome and suave as he was, belonged to Juliet. And also he was interdimensionally unavailable. The switchboard room's handsome scanner voice was invisible, and most assuredly too young. Most men were too young.

Something was wrong somewhere, no one necessarily knew where, but certainly Juliet knew, is what Sabine finally came away with.

Similarly, Juliet's search for homes where people left their porch lights on during the day, began in 1961 after an intense study of Michelangelo Antonioni's *La Notte* made her realize that if she couldn't find her soul family, she could always join the family of the disaffected. A bond was a bond, it didn't matter what you called it.

But her deep fear remained: What if all the myths that helped her were based on nothing but shadows? This was incited by Fermi's Paradox, which she translated as *Where Is Everybody?*

Thus she believed she had been placed in Trauma Town to rekindle her marriage with Tristan, no matter who was in what quantum state at any moment.

However, Juliet was not able to actually experience a space where everyone could be together. A gathering space. Within the oneness she knew theoretically was there, there was just ... her.

Still, she trusted that something must be somewhere at some point. Armed with her Chopra-confirmed non-local mind-set, Juliet felt somewhat confident and possibly semi-validated.

"About ready to go?" Juliet's voice was breathless.

Sabine thought Juliet had intentionally suppressed the question mark at the end in order to calm herself down. "Absolutely."

Sabine had no problem with the fact that she was totally not ready to go, because she had learned from Juliet that everything was relative and words were simply symbolic fragments of poorly understood concepts - floating utterances that could mean anything, depending on the tone and the moment.

From deep inside an interior wall in the switchboard room at Telecomm, a muffled pager beeped, as Sabine and Juliet stood by the switchboard room door buttoning up their winter coats. Sabine had tried a new hair glue that morning in an attempt to keep her 1960s straight cut bangs from getting frizzy.

She had not found hair glue in Juliet's bathroom when she had looked through all the drawers and cabinets, so she was working the bangs blind, without confirmation, although she remembered that Juliet's bathroom smelled like hydrangea candles and new shower curtain liner. And all there was in the medicine cabinet were just a few staples: Caviar Anti-aging Shampoo and Christophe Robin *pâte lavante volumisante au rassoul pur et extraits de rose*, which Sabine assumed was hair conditioner.

The pager was still beeping. "There's a mouse stuck in the wall," Juliet murmured, her loose golden hair moving in slow motion as she scanned the switchboard room.

Aja was seated at her operator's station, swatting away unseen flying insects.

Nyx leaned against Aja's workspace, exuding Avon *Exotic Nights* and accidentally detonating the automated hospital-wide announcement system, telling people not to walk through the fire doors during a drill. "I just dusted all these counters yesterday, Aja."

Raphael stood in the back by the engineer's desk, legs a combo, tablet and stylus in hand, ready to capture the moment, should one arise.

Yanina was just outside the open Telecomm door, lit by a buzzing fluorescent hall light, her phone at her ear just in case someone called, and her other hand balancing an open laptop.

Sabine felt the electrical currents going through everyone and felt her heart indulge in a momentary arrhythmia.

"Me too, I'm ready to go." Glo stood up from her station as Valentine, Tashuna, and Wing swooped in to take over the shift. "So Sabine, you have the deciphered files? Yes?"

"Oh my dear dear Glo, you have no idea."

"Nor do I want to," Glo said. "But where? I don't see any files, I don't see any tote with stuff in it, like, where are they?"

Sabine reached into a side pocket of her winter pink extra-large tote from 31, pulled out a tiny USB flash drive, and held it up like it was a bottle of Screaming Eagle Cabernet Sauvignon.

"Alright then," Glo said. "We're all toast. We're toast. I knew it." Through the ghostly green lighting of the switchboard room, flecked with occasional stabs from the hall fluorescent, Sabine saw Glo rolling her eyes.

"Go already," said Wing. "We're trying to answer the phones here, alright?"

"Sabine, you can't just use any old USB stick," said Yanina, "It's non-compliant. All electronics have to be run through BioMed before they can be brought into the building." Yanina gestured to make her point, dropped her phone, and watched in slow motion as it smashed into a number of pieces on the linoleum. "Oh toads," she said. "Now look what you've made me do. Sabine I know now why they fired you, you have pervasive compliance issues."

"You need to worship the compliance gods with more gusto," Glo translated.

"Thank you for calling Trummel Hospital, this is Wing," cut through the crowd in a overly loud voice.

"Way to break someone's eardrum," Glo muttered toward Yunky. "Raphael, you're awfully quiet. You must know something."

"Yes officer," Wing said. "A Status 1 impalement? Yes okay, I'll let Lulu know it's coming in."

"I do," Raphael said. "Or at least I kind of do. We'll improvise once we're at the party and see what happens."

"I saw the party room," said Nyx. She had let her hair down for the occasion, and coincidentally it was the same color and style as Juliet's hair. "Denize was so grateful to the Trummel Rehab people that she organized the party in the rehab building gym."

"You have a Status 1 impalement coming in," Wing said into her headset microphone. "Yes. Something to do with a ski pole... Alright." Wing turned in her chair to face the general populace. "Lulu can't make it to the party," she announced.

Oddly, Denize's release day from rehab coincided exactly with Clea's release from the Program Unit Facility.

Denize was finally able to eat Dairy Queen, so the insurance company gave her a discharge.

Clea's daily visitor at the psych unit, Victor from Trauma Town Security, who had an impeccable record of saving innocent young girls, had written a long letter to Henry Moho vouching for Clea's mental health, so PUF discharged her. Yanina signed off on it, since Clea had no insurance.

So Denize and Nicole from the rehab, had organized a farewell good luck party, with Glo at the helm of food and entertainment, Sabine and Juliet in charge of finding people to come to the party, and

Raphael covering it for the front page of the *Trummel Sun*. Raphael had been promised a by-line in bold and he was stoked. If he could uncover something, anything, this could be his ticket back to the East Village.

The gym at Trummel Rehab was animated with a strobe created by a complex system of malfunctioning overhead lights. The gym equipment had been pushed against the walls to make more room for partygoers, with purple crepe paper and blinking white party lights strung from weight racks and leg presses, through stands of large, colorful exercise balls, over a rebounder, and through treadmill handlebars.

Glo had placed speakers in each corner of the gym, and Maz, who had regained consciousness, had flown in Bent Fabric from Cincinnati to do their hit song, *Keep On Rising.*

The room was packed and noisy.

"This reminds me of a Broadway cast after opening night, getting together at Sardi's to congratulate each other and wait for the reviews to hit the papers," Juliet said to Sabine as they walked in, flanked by Glo, Raphael, Nyx, Aja, and Yanina.

"It looks like the whole cast is here," Sabine answered. She was surprised at the large crowd - from

Lile the condo maintenance guy to Karina, the owner of the Black Cat, Dr. Raj, who was evidently not helping Lulu with the Status 1 impalement, a covey of handsome Valley Ambulance paramedics still in uniform, Sunami the night nurse on Three who helped Julian Boulevard cling to the planet until his wife could get there to say goodbye, and anyone from the Park View Nursing home who was mobile. Apparently people had come, despite the fact that Sabine and Juliet never did get the word out. "This is Trummel. Word spreads superluminally," Juliet had explained to Sabine.

Bent Fabric was tuning up on a small platform under the basketball hoop at the far end of the gym. There was only the one basketball hoop because no one at Trummel rehab was well enough to play basketball. Heavy winter coats and backpacks were strewn against the walls, and people were buzzing about.

"I'm sensing a massive galvanic arc running crisscross underneath the wooden floor and shooting up into everyone through their shoes," Juliet said.

"Oh my God, Juliet, me too!" said Raphael, quickly assessing whether Juliet even heard him. "Total electricity," he tried again, then sighed and went back to his tablet.

"This is like the night Denize got shot," Sabine said to Juliet and their little group. "Remember? Everyone acted as a team with just one focus. Back then it was to save Denize's life. And now ... now it's ..."

The little group fell silent amid the echoey rumble of the crowd, thinking of what it might be.

"Is the meteorite here yet?" Yanina's voice projected a powerful soprano formant that broke the group's concentration. "Nothing is covered if an act of God happens. Hello, acts of God? Why would God create an act of God? Am I right?"

"Hold that thought, Yunky," Glo shouted in a loud whisper to the Telecomm group. "We have an Incoming."

They were just inside the gym entrance. Glo had donned a wireless headset that evening just in case the handsome scanner guy should materialize - the wireless being a sign of coolness and high tech which Glo knew was attractive to millennials - and it was buried under her thick, grayish brown hair, flashing on and off. Every time it flashed on, the left side of her face turned green.

And then Henry Moho molecularized into the middle of the crowded gym like a ghost squeezing onto a rush hour Manhattan subway car. He made his way through the crowd to Bent Fabric's platform and tapped the microphone to make sure it was working. "Good evening, people," he said in a low, god-like, inflectionless voice when the room was quiet. "As you all know, well, anyway, alright, I'm not one to side step an issue. Here it is. I heard that the files - I mean 'The Files' have been decrypted."

Echoey silence. It was unclear to Sabine whether the sudden quiet was because no one had any idea what Henry was talking about, or because no one actually cared. She left her group and made her way to the platform to join Henry. She, too, tapped a found microphone. "Henry, that would be a yes with some additional backstory."

The Telecomm group also migrated toward the platform. "I'm concerned about any copyright issues," Sabine heard Yunky say to Raphael. "Put that in your article so we're covered."

"Any copyright on these files expired a few generations ago," Raphael said.

A handsome middle-aged man stepped up onto the now crowded little platform with Sabine and Henry. Sabine didn't recognize him at first because he was healthy, but she realized it was Maz. He politely confiscated a Bent Fabric backup singer microphone, cleared his throat, and straightened his tie.

"Henry," Sabine said as Maz fiddled with the microphone's on/off switch. She held up her USB memory stick so everyone could see it. "This is what you've been looking for." Her voice echoed - someone from the band had turned on the reverb. "It was never just a file - it's a manuscript. An ancient, original manuscript. From 1871 -"

Maz got his microphone turned on. "To see Bent Fabric's upcoming concert schedule, just go to their website. I urge everyone to check it out." He put the mike back in the stand, apparently done, and started talking into his watch.

Henry put his mike back in its stand, and turned to look at Sabine. She switched her mike off in response. "That's what it is, Henry. The paper files with all the codes and numbers - they were hiding the manuscript."

The crowd retreated back into its groups and picked up where they left off. Henry and Sabine stepped off the platform. Maz, now distracted by some disturbing text messaging, joined them.

"I don't know about this, Sabine," Henry said. "I was explicitly told that there was an urgent message in the paper files. Something that could save the hospital from being bought out by ExxonMobil."

"ExxonMobil?"

"One of those. Maybe it was Johnson and Johnson. They make band aids. That's their connection to healthcare."

"No, it's nothing like that, Henry," Sabine said. "It's a manuscript. Like, a found manuscript. I've read it - it's -"

"Henry, it's urgent," Juliet said. "It was written by my third great grandmother for her doctoral thesis."

"Her doctoral thesis," Raphael emphasized. He was holding his micro mini tablet in one hand, his stylus in the other.

Maz returned his attention to the group, loosened his tie - he and Henry were the only men in the room wearing suits. Sabine was glad Maz was part of her little group because his strange dress validated his importance.

"I actually acquired the rights to the manuscript," Maz said. "That's why I was in Trummel when I had my stroke. I had to go to some sort of stroke induced connection to get it, but I got it."

Nyx turned to look at Maz, as if seeing him for the first time. "I'm Nyx," she said. Maz smiled and Nyx blushed.

"Henry, this is it, it's now or never, this or nothing," said Glo. "I've seen the manuscript. It has the potential to -"

Henry sighed dramatically. "Bottom line. How will this get Trummel Hospital out of its financial entanglement?"

"It's big picture, Henry," Juliet said. "But it starts at the quantum level. You remember, I'm sure, the quantum foam discovery in 1955? So if you have a financial shortage, all you have to do is entangle it with a financial windfall."

"Ah - no, I don't think so," Raphael said. "I've done this research with you, and I don't think we can draw that conclusion. We'd have to read the manuscript again to get a better picture."

"Wouldn't a shortage and a windfall cancel each other out?" said Aja.

"What Juliet means," said Sabine, "is that it's possible to harness the power of the mind to … hmm, it came and went, now I don't know."

"It's too noisy here," said Nyx. "Let's go down the hall to the reception station."

"The copyright is clear," Yanina said as the group migrated through the crowd to the gym entrance and down the hall to the front desk. Yunky had been wearing high heeled boots, but the left heel had broken off somewhere between the hospital and the gym, and she was alternating between five foot six and five foot four with each step. "If the manuscript is from 1871, it's in the public domain."

They passed a couple walking the other way, toward the party. "Well yes, I was a little shell-shocked, but nothing out of the ordinary," one was saying.

And then Sabine stopped short and forgot to breathe.

Seated at the front desk was Denize, her now short pixie hair a brilliant dark purple. Propped up on the counter in front of her was Clea. The two were having an animated discussion. Clea was wearing a cotton flowered maxi-dress and swinging her fleece-lined wafflestompers casually, and neither one was trying to kill the other.

Without missing a beat, Raphael hoisted himself up onto the counter next to Clea. "Ladies, you probably know who I am," he said. In New York he had a Press Badge that he bought online, but he lost it in the move to Trummel.

Clea and Denize looked at him with blank but accepting smiles.

"I mean, if you read the paper," Raphael said. "I write for the paper. They put my picture by my articles. Sometimes." He pulled his mini tablet out of his oversized L.L. Bean flannel shirt side pocket.

Denize smiled. "That's nice."

Clea inched closer to him. "You're a writer!"

Raphael lowered his voice. "Why yes, yes I am."

"What types of things do you write?" Clea said. "My great great great, or something, aunt - or maybe she was a cousin - was a writer."

"So was mine," said Denize.

"Have I ever read your stuff?" said Clea. Her right side was leaning against his left side and the excess fabric from her long skirt fell across his left knee.

From inside the gym, Sabine heard Bent Fabric begin playing. She recognized the song from her *Le Freak by Chic* playlist as *Early Morning in Copenhagen.* "This is making me nervous," she whispered to Juliet.

"Damn, me too," said Glo.

"I feel that we need to check for weapons," answered Juliet.

"I forgot to put the spinach in my celery smoothie this morning," said Aja.

Clea looked over at the group and locked eyes with Sabine. Her smile turned down and large tears suddenly dripped down her cheeks. She hopped off the counter and took Sabine's hands in hers. Sabine breathed in the patchouli and froze.

"It was an accident, Sabine," Clea said in her high-pitched, thin child voice. "I'm so sorry, really. Really." She shook their hands up and down as if to break Sabine's stunned trance. "I was just having an awful day." Clea blinked back tears. "Surely you understand. My stress level was unbearable, I've always been, well they use the term delicate, always have been since I was little. I have a cortisol imbalance. I come from a broken family. I never knew my mother."

Dumbstruck, Sabine felt obligated to say something. "Oh it's okay."

"Thank you, thank you!" Clea let go of Sabine's hands and danced back to Raphael. "Oh - or my father," she said, now smiling again.

"We're cousins," Denize explained to the group. "Kind of, somehow."

"Yes," Clea said. My great great great Aunt Indigo wrote a manuscript for her doctoral thesis detailing the secret history of the song *Row Row Row Your Boat*."

"She had to go undercover into a secret society," added Denize. "But she was able to get the true history of this song."

"Its provenance," said Clea. "And she said it was to go to her great great niece, should this great great niece ever surface."

"I thought I had found it, although I didn't know what it was," said Denize. "I met Henry Moho and I knew something was going on."

"It was supposed to go to me," Clea said, her smile gone and her voice oddly grown-up.

"No, Clea," said Denize. "Remember, we talked about this? You agreed that great-aunt Indigo didn't realize she had two nieces? Remember? You said you could handle this if you knew the truth."

Aja was pacing across the rehab front entrance, causing the automatic doors to open and close every minute or so.

Maz and Nyx had gone missing.

Raphael took Clea's hand as if to keep her from falling. "Careful, there," he mumbled to justify.

Juliet floated over to the counter. "I have it." Her voice was rich, warm, and textured - as if she was sipping a rare port by a calm shore in Fiji under a full moon. Clea and Denize just looked at her, speechless and hypnotized. Juliet's loose, blond messy Parisian hair sparkled, and her body-hugging, sequined nude and black cut-out floor-length evening gown made her look like an exotic high priestess. She gently leaned down to give Denize a small hug, and then leaned over and took Clea's hand. "I have the manuscript. Or Sabine might have it. But no matter. I'm feeling like I might be beginning to find my people," she said, looking from Clea to Denize.

Sabine saw a soft golden glow radiate from Juliet's smile.

Chapter 17

Sabine's DNA was altered in her grade
school chorus when they sang Dello Joio's *A
Jubilant Song*, with lyrics from Walt Whitman's
Leaves of Grass. Singing this piece, with its
difficult harmonies and soaring lyrics, she felt
that at some point, she should be able to fly. She
was still waiting.

Juliet's DNA was altered upon hearing
Bach's *Mass in B Minor* - a piece of consummate
optimism - when she was too young to defend
herself.

Henry's mike went back on. "People. Your
attention, please, sometime before next Christmas.
There are deadlines looming."

No one was listening. Bent Fabric was playing
Nattens sidste cigaret - Last Night's Cigarette - so
Henry turned his volume up.

"People. Your jobs may have been totally
saved." The crowd's sudden silence was punctuated
with two seconds of microphone feedback. Bent Fabric
stopped playing, mainly because they were squeezed
off the stage. Henry vibrated into and out of sight for a
second, and then regained his composure. "My friend

Maz here from Cincinnati has broken the code that will bring Trummel Hospital - and Trummel itself - back to prosperity - and by that of course I mean back to being able to serve the community better."

"Henry, for heaven's sake," Sabine said into her reverberating microphone. "Maz is awesome, to be sure, just even for coming back from the, uh, the, um, the other side."

"I was dead," Maz said.

"There's really no such thing as death," Sabine said. "You're here, and then you're there. Is that really such a big deal."

"I was there and now I'm here," Maz said.

"Anyway, I was there too and I came back here with this manuscript, but I must give credit to Juliet Indigo - you all know Juliet, right?"

The crowd pulsated with a silent flumoxity.

"My friend Juliet. We all need to thank her, it was her third great grandmother who wrote this manuscript that Maz, with his alchemy skills, will turn into gold."

Lile, the maintenance/pizza delivery guy at the condo, stepped up onto the tiny stage wearing his usual outfit of baggy shorts and a navy blue hoodie which he wore year-round regardless of the weather. "A round of applause, Trummelites, right? Yes? Am I right? Trummel is once again to be the bustling, busy hub that it might have ever been?"

The crowd broke into a sincere applause. Then someone shouted, "What's in the manuscript?" Someone else shouted, "Who is Juliet?" And another shout, "Play *One More For the Road.*"

A pocket of people by the resistance balls promptly broke into the song. "*Make it one for my baby and one more for the road.*"

A Bent Fabric guitar player with a gray man ponytail squeezed back onto the platform and whispered into Sabine's ear. "We need to play music, it's who we are. Can you guys take this somewhere else?"

"This is what I'm going to put in the article," said Raphael. "I do not have an ego. Tell me exactly your exact opinion, okay?"

The Black Cat was empty except for the small Telecomm covey. The rest of the town was still partying at Trummel Rehab.

Raphael and Henry put four wobbly wooden tables together, and Nyx and Yanina grabbed chairs from around the room and dragged them over.

"The headline," continued Raphael over Glo whispering loudly about having missed dinner, Aja calling "I know you're in there somewhere" into the dark expanse of her tote, and various chair adjustment scraping noises.

The makeshift Black Cat conference table looked out onto Trummel's Main Street, lit with pools of streetlamps. A gentle sleet tapping the big front window served as background music.

"I'm listening, Raphael," said Henry.

"Okay." Raphael rumpled his thick, curly hair nervously with one hand, while he read from his tablet. "The headline. 300 year-old doctoral thesis discovered. Or maybe it should be uncovered."

"Discovered is good," Sabine said.

"It wasn't discovered," Denize said. "It always existed. It was uncovered."

"It was supposed to be mine," Clea said.

"It's ours, Clea," Denize said. "And Juliet's."

"Actually it's mine," Maz said. "I purchased the rights to it, remember?"

"Damn it, Denize."

Clea and Denize were sitting in the same chair. Neither was about to move, although each one looked like she might slip off at any moment.

"Hey, guys, I'm still reading you my article," said Raphael.

Glo appeared from behind the bar and plopped a large bowl of pretzels onto the tables at exactly the same time that Maz put his elbows on it as perhaps a power gesture. The whole thing wobbled, and the pretzels toppled through the resulting crack between the tables and fell onto the floor. Nyx and Yanina pushed the tables back together without missing a beat, during which time Juliet broke out her compact and dabbed powder on her nose to make sure there was no shine.

"That's really excellent, Raphael," said Juliet in a low, confident mistress of ceremonies voice. "Sabine, can you give everyone the details?"

"It's an ancient, original manuscript," said Sabine, after everyone had retrieved their respective wines and beers from behind the bar. Raphael sat down and began typing self-consciously on his tablet. "It was written by Juliet's third great grandmother Indigo in 1871 and it detailed the provenance of the mysterious children's song, *Row Row Row Your Boat*."

"*Row Row Row Your Boat*?" said Henry. "Sabine, dear girl, tell me you've started our little meeting with a funny joke. Maz is here from Cincinnati, he doesn't have time for funny jokes."

"Life is but a dream," said Aja who had ended up next to Henry. "Everyone knows that."

Clea and Denize were still sharing the same chair. "That's what was the main agenda for her doctoral thesis. Life is but a dream," Clea said.

"Our great great great aunt had to go undercover into a secret society to get this information," added Denize.

'Life is but a dream?" echoed Yanina. "How is that possible? I'm sitting here holding an actual wine glass with actual wine in it. If you pinch me, I will feel it."

"Alright, people, let's totally get real here. The manuscript is real, it's been verified. Right, Maz?" said Henry.

Maz looked up from his Google watch as if caught by a teacher passing a love note to a girl, albeit many years ago. "Yes, of course, verified, yes."

"Just because the manuscript says Life is but a dream doesn't mean that it is," said Henry. "It just means that it's an ancient original manuscript that's been discovered."

Henry's wine glass was emptying, but Sabine never saw him take a sip. "I do miss the taste of pinot noir," he mumbled. "But never mind." His voice filled the room again. "Sabine?"

"Yes?"

"My dear, you've had these files for weeks now," Henry said. "And except for getting shot in the head, you've had every opportunity to come up with something that will bring the hospital back from financial ruin. Not *Row Row Row Your Boat*."

Raphael stood up, emboldened by his imminent escape from Trummel and possible triumphant return to the East Village. "I've already verified the provenance, Henry. What Sabine has on her USB memory stick is an absolute gold mine. A Trummel treasure."

Juliet was seated between Sabine and Raphael. She had re-applied her makeup and cleared the black globs from underneath her eyes with a Q-tip from her makeup bag. "My Grandmother Indigo was a scholar." Her soft, alto voice was breathy but its *tenuto* uncharacteristically emphasized each word.

Henry sat down. "I apologize, Miss Juliet," he said. "You're right, of course. She was a scholar."

"You… knew her?" Juliet said.

"Why yes, yes I did. Or, I do. She was a great lady. Ahead of her time. She had a thing for tardigrades."

"Yes of course, thank you, Henry," Juliet replied.

Henry smiled. Sabine had never seen such a thing.

The Black Cat was quiet except for the sound of sleet hitting the window.

Juliet took a deep breath and made gentle eye contact with each person around the table. "So - Maz and I have been talking." Her dusky voice and softly glowing aura filled the little café.

As Juliet began speaking, Sabine realized that the world, looked at holistically, had the potential to be a safe place for her cats.

Maz gulped some froth from the top of his mug of Smooth Hoperator. Nyx, to his left, sipped a spritzer.

"It turns out - thank you, Miss Juliet - ". Maz kind of bowed to Juliet, across the table. "Great great great grandmother Indigo went undercover into a secret society to get this story."

"It's a secret history," Raphael interjected, reading from his tablet.

"It's a mysterious but true history of the song," Juliet said.

"And I've been - well, my career was taking a downward turn," said Maz, "but anyway - my friend Nyx has filled me in on the details of this opportunity, and I've decided to make a comeback."

Aja had given up on finding whatever she was looking for in her tote, and concentrated instead on her virgin tomato juice. "Very happy for you," she said with some effort, as if appearing present.

"Yes, I'm going to make the discovery into a mind-blowing documentary," said Maz. "Well first of course there will be the book rights, but then the documentary rights."

"What's the documentary about?" said Aja.

"It's about the secret history of the song *Row Row Row Your Boat*," said Raphael. "Silly girl, he just said that."

"Based of course on Grandmother Indigo's doctoral thesis," Maz continued. "I think it's fabulous. My vision is to be the next mogul or possibly the next Ken Burns. Excuse me I have to make a phone call." He took a sip of his beer. "Dave?" He yelled into his watch. "Dave? Get down here immediately, we have a deal, this is going to be huge. Alright, then up here, whatever."

"It's up," said Yanina.

Maz turned to look at Yanina as if seeing her for the first time. "You have an uncanny attention to detail," he said. "I will be needing a secretary as I get this project off the ground. The job's yours if you want it."

"I too have skills," said Nyx. "What I mean is, Yunky can't leave. She's the utilization review nurse."

The chair holding Denize and Clea fell backward as its left back leg snapped off. The girls fell to the floor in a twist of long flowered dresses, complicated scarves, and surprised screams.

"Right on, troopers," said Glo. "Way to share a chair."

Denize and Clea began laughing uncontrollably, got up and went over to the front door to get their coats from the coat rack. By the time they were buttoned up and leaving, they were bent over from laughing, and out of breath trying to talk to each other at the same time. Their departure left a silence, filled by the rhythmic thudding of melty ice pellets against the picture window. Everyone sipped their drinks. Glo crunched a pretzel.

Juliet smiled at Henry like a patient teacher working with a beloved but distracted student. "Aren't you forgetting something, Henry?"

Henry looked at her blankly for a second, and then, as if picking up information telepathically, said, "Oh. Yes of course. Goodness. Um, Sabine."

"Yes sir?"

"You're re-hired. I had your Incident File demolecularized."

The switchboard room was the same as it ever was. Glo had a small tablet with a speaker she had placed in the back of the room on the engineer's desk, from which Talking Heads sang *Once in a Lifetime*.

Sabine, in a dark burgundy evening gown she got at Nordstrom's in 1996 during some sort of red-wine-induced manic high, had her headset on, even though the earphones pierced into her rhinestone dangling earrings and made her ears itch. "Thank you for calling Trummel - what?"

"Yes dear. I told Ethel, watch out because she, I mean, someone killed my husband you know, the cars. Oh watch out, they're under the tunnel, I mean, with um. underpants. I can't find Ethel."

"Shall I put you through to the Emergency Room, m'am?"

"I suppose so."

Sabine forwarded the call to Lulu.

"I hope to God he comes back," Glo said, sitting at her station next to Sabine and donning her headset. "Then you'll believe me that he really was here."

"Who? Oh, gosh I don't care about that," said Sabine.

"That's why you're wearing an evening gown and dangling rhinestone earrings," Glo said. "Because you don't care."

"Glo, I'm on the phone."

"He's too young, I'm telling you."

His voice crooned over the scanner. *"Psychiatric emergency, Delta Level. Man threatening to jump into, ah, Milky Way's black hole. 10 Vine Street at Mister Muffler's. All units respond."*

The door opened a crack. "Hey guys, are you busy?"

"There's only two of us here, now, Aja," said Glo. "You have left the dark cave for a better cave and more pay."

Aja smiled as she tiptoed in, closed the door behind her, and sat at her old station.

"Do you miss us?" said Sabine.

"I do," said Aja. "I'm totally out of my league as the new utilization review nurse. The good news of the promotion and pay raise has given me PTSD. But Henry doesn't seem to care, what with the huge influx of money from Maz and his machine."

"There's something I've been debating whether or not to tell you," said Glo.

Aja picked up her old head set and fondled it. "What?"

"I mean, keep this quiet, but you're supposed to have a nursing degree to be a utilization review nurse. Nurse, being the operative word."

"Henry's putting me through night school. I get to work daytimes now, and go to school at night."

"Way to work days and nights," Glo said.

"Makes me exhausted just thinking about it," said Sabine.

"I'm going to simplify the utilization review system," said Aja. "Nyx is helping me. We're going to allow anyone to have whatever coverage they need in order to get well."

Glo let out a sharp laugh. "We're going to save your switchboard work station for you. Just in case, you know."

"You'll be fine, Aja," said Sabine.

"Also I'm starting over. I need to pull myself together, I'm over it," said Aja.

"Over what?" said Glo.

"Oh for heaven sakes, Glo, everything. I'm starting fresh. I'm going to take a biofeedback course to try to re-claim my brain. Also get back into shape physically."

"That's excellent, Aja," said Sabine.

"It feels good. Every day I do my workout for abs, thighs, and butt."

Glo was off the phone. "Every day I do my workout for hernia, pelvic floor, and vertigo. Never miss a day."

Aja laughed and left the cave for her new office two doors down.

The two-way radio crackled and Victor's voice said, *"Security to switchboard, come in."*

Glo and Sabine both grabbed for the radio, but Sabine pulled back to answer another call.

"Switchboard here," said Glo.

"We have an active Code Orange, third floor in the lab," Victor said.

"Hold one moment," Sabine said to her caller, and switched on the hold button. She turned to Glo.

"Copy, Victor," said Glo.

"Do you copy?" said Victor.

"Yes I copy," said Glo. "What's going on up there on Three?"

"Not sure yet," said Victor, *"but I'm thinking chemical spill."*

"What chemical, Victor?" said Glo.

"I'm thinking sodium azide."

"What's that?"

"No idea. That word was flying around." Victor's voice lowered with conspiratorial excitement. *"Dr. Raj was in the morgue using it to preserve some slides he found on Mr. Boulevard's autopsy. He's proving the existence of the new Black Widow virus, the key to bacteria as we know it."* Victor cleared his throat and went back to professional security voice. *"Call the code, stat. Over and out."*

For the briefest moment, Sabine and Glo looked at each other without moving. Then they both lunged for the desk microphone, which Nyx had moved to the engineer's desk last time she dusted. Glo was limping from a recent issue with her new hip, and Sabine, lurching for the mike, fell off her 4 inch heels and grabbed her chair, which twirled around. Glo fell onto the microphone, knocking it to the floor, and Sabine fell on the mike as her left foot fell out of her shoe.

"Attention all personnel," Sabine said from the floor, holding the microphone like a prize. "Code Orange in the lab, Level Three. Code Orange in the lab, Level Three."

"I'm alright," Glo said, falling into her workstation chair.

"Sorry about that, Glo." Sabine handed the microphone up to Glo. "Fight or flight, or something. Took over me."

Glo laughed nervously as she took the mike and wiped floor dirt off the front of her pullover. "Ah me. Life in the fast lane."

Sabine pulled herself up, and sat at her workstation. "We'd better get the flash emails out and set up a command center." Her eyes rested briefly on a post-it note in a forgotten corner of the bulletin board that had been there since she her first day, fifteen years ago. "Plants watered on Wed." Some Wednesday, fifteen years ago, some plant was watered.

"Yes yes yes. Life in the Buddha Chillout Lounge."

The switchboard room door opened and Aja popped her head in. "Sodium azide spill on Three! Dr. Raj poured it down the sink. Tom from Facilities corroborated that the sinks in the lab still have copper pipes, and we are fried." She closed the door and Sabine heard her running down the hall.

A second later the door opened again and Tom from Facilities poked his head in. "Alright ladies, I'll say this once because I'm on a mission. The stuff Dr. Raj poured down the sink in the lab has turned into some sort of solution with some sort of serious hospital-wide inhalation hazard." And he was gone.

"Did you get the flash email out?" said Glo.

"Yes, the flash email went out," said Sabine.

"What do we do now?" said Glo.

"I guess follow protocol, right? What else is there?" said Sabine.

"Protocol it is," said Glo.

"We'll go down with the ship," said Sabine.

"There's nothing else to do," affirmed Glo.

"Has anyone responded to the code?" said Sabine.

"Not that I can tell," said Glo, "but then who am I, right? Maybe they responded and just didn't confirm it with us, the Command Center."

"Who might respond?" said Sabine.

"The responders," said Glo. "Don't you worry one ounce about this, my dear little one-shoe Sabine. And they were indeed fabulous shoes, until they weren't. There are specific people who respond to specific codes. The heroes are probably on their way."

Sabine knew Glo was right. There were knowledgeable people in well-fitted dark uniforms with specialized training. She leaned back in her chair and took a deep breath, as her body relaxed and she thought about rescued cats. She was at home again. Back at work. In the warm familiarity of a crisis.

Chapter 18

Sabine never got over a certain warm breeze she felt at dusk one night, dancing on Copacabana Beach at Carnival, with her very first husband who died young, the man who thought she was fabulous.

Sabine raced home from the hospital, ripped off the chiffon evening gown she had work to work, kicked her high heels off in different directions, poured a glass of Merlot, pulled the comforter back on her bed and climbed in.

"Love loves," she called to her flock. "We're in bed, I need the tribe of fur." She went into a falsetto grandmother voice: "Kitties? I need the kitties. On the bed. Stat." Freddie, Dr. Crusher, and Higgs-Boson came from their hiding places and jumped onto the bed. "Awww. Hello, little angels."

Three loud purrings and three deeply happy entities padded around the bed. Dr. Crusher put her little wet nose onto Sabine's nose. Sabine felt the sweet tiger breath on her cheek. Freddie aggressively pumped his claws into the thick comforter, and Higgs turned upside down so Sabine could rub her warm tummy.

Sabine took a deep sip of her wine, and reached over to her nightstand, placing the delicate glass on *The Star Trek Book: Strange New Worlds Boldly Explained* by Paul Ruditis. Next to her book and wine was a vintage lamp with a ruffled shade from the Walmart shabby chic collection. She had recently changed the lightbulb from white to soft yellow, giving her bedroom a velvety, amber glow.

The question floated gently through Sabine's mind: Why didn't Jean-Paul hang out with me after he died, the way Tristan stayed with Juliet?

For further intel on this issue, she picked up her cell phone and tapped the speed-dial for Juliet. It rang three times and went to voicemail. She hung up, took another sip of wine, and pressed re-dial. Three rings and voicemail again. Her cozy safe place was a breath away from disintegrating. She pressed re-dial a third time. Panic was making her toes twitch and was moving up through her body --- but then Juliet picked up.

"*Sweetie!*" Juliet said.

"Juliet, thank God," Sabine said.

"*Hi, sweetie.*"

"Hi, Juliet, hi and hello. Hi."

Juliet's voice sounded farther away than usual, and Sabine pressed her phone more tightly against her ear so she wouldn't miss anything.

"Job well done, Sabine!" said Juliet. *"You are incredible. You brought the hospital back from its endgame. You know you're a hero, right?"*

"I'm a hero?"

Juliet laughed, and Sabine heard music in the background. It was *Celebrate* by Kool & The Gang.

Sabine remembered hearing that song with Jean-Paul, her very first husband who adored her, when they were in Rio for their honeymoon thirty-five years before. She felt the warmth of the Brazilian summer, tasted the sugary lime of the caipirinhas, the national drink, and she remembered their first night there.

The windows were open and Sabine and Jean-Paul listened to music playing from the streets. Lights from a cruise ship lit up the windowsill where they saw a small lizard make its way into their room. It had an orchid in its mouth. "Our little lizard is a vegetarian," Jean-Paul said, delighted. Sabine lay awake all that night, because her gratitude was too visceral to sleep.

"I hear music," she said to Juliet.

"Oh Sabine, I wish you were here. Why aren't you here?"

"Where?"

"Oh - um, I think we're in New York somewhere. Clea and Denize and I drove to New York. We're at the Copacabana Times Square."

"Oh, that's wonderful Juliet. You've found your people."

"What's that?" The music and crowd noises were making it hard to hear.

"I can hardly hear you, Juliet."

"Sweetie, what? I can't hear you."

From her voiceover days, Sabine knew how to project her voice. She went to a lower timbre and more volume. "Stuff is working for you, Juliet. You've found your people."

"Hang on -"

Sabine heard muffled laughter over the music.

"Okay, I'm back. Enough dancing. We had to have a group hug."

"You sound good, Juliet. You sound … happy. Not so wistful, right? Happy? Dancing and hugging?"

Juliet laughed. *"Staying hydrated, my dear."*

Sabine reached for the vintage nightstand lamp and clicked the yellow light off and on and off and on again. "Hydrated. Yes, me too."

"I wish you had come with us. The city is bright and alive, Sabine."

The fact that Sabine didn't even know they were going to New York was not an issue. She was actually relieved that she wasn't given the choice to go. She knew when her shift was over at the hospital that night, that she had to just rush home, grab the wine, throw her clothes off and sink into her soft bed with the cats. A trip to New York would have interfered with this. "When are you coming back?"

"Me and Clea and Denize got the most amazing check from Maz, Sabine. A royalty check."

"Really? Oh that's wonderful! Wow, Juliet. So happy for you guys." Sabine felt a wave of delight rush through her. She realized in that moment that Juliet's melancholy had taken a toll on her. Juliet finding her life's dream - a family - after what she had been through with Tristan - was yet another confirmation that things were going to be okay for her also.

"You, my dear," Juliet said. *"You, you you."*

"No, Juliet. This is your day. My heart is bursting with joy for you guys." Sabine was sipping her Merlot more quickly than she thought she should. But it felt good - like a celebration. She'd pay for it tomorrow with a headache, but it was worth it for the momentary high.

Amid the background noise, Sabine heard the end of *Celebrate* and the start of *All Day and All of the Night* by the Kinks.

"How are the kitties?" Juliet said. Her words were slurring slightly.

294 / Suzann Kale

"They send their love. They say thank you for taking care of them after I got shot."

"They send their love. They say thank you for taking care of them after I got shot."

"Give each one a kiss for me, okay Sabine?"

"Okay, Juliet."

"Good bye, sweet little neighbor."

"Bye, Juliet. Love you." Sabine pushed the red end button on her phone. She felt good. Her panic had gone away. She could just push a button on her phone and talk to Juliet any time she needed to, whether or not Juliet ever came back from New York.

"Raphael."

"Hey. Sabine."

"I'm drunk dialing again."

"I know. You okay?"

"Oh God, yes. You?"

"Hell yes."

"Are you in New York, too?"

"On my way, I think. Nothing certain, but yeah. I think."

"Are you going back to the East Village?"

"Oh my god, heaven be praised, manna coming from the mountains."

"That's awesome."

"Why don't you come with me, Sabine? You could get a telecommunications job at one of the Manhattan hospitals, you'd be perfect. They'd love you."

"Really?"

"Of course. You could stay with me until you scored a gig."

"Really, Raphael?"

"Jesus, Sabine, yes. Really. With your experience, you'd have a job in no time. And now you can get references. From Henry, from everyone."

"Henry hasn't been around in a while, Raphael."

"Okay, from HR, from Glo. Now that Aja is a utilization review nurse, have her write up a referral for you, it would have clout. You are not staying in Trauma Town."

Sabine heard *Native New Yorker* by Odyssey playing in Raphael's background. "I have three cats."

"Sabine. Bring the damn cats. I'm freaking serious. What's wrong with you?"

"What if one of them, like, gets out? In New York, I'd never find them again."

"Oh, okay. So - here's what we do. Put down the Merlot."

"The Merlot and the cats are non-negotiable."

There was a long pause. *"I love you, Sabine, you know that."*

"I love you, too, Raphael."

"You belong in New York."

296 / Suzann Kale

"I know. Oh - gotta go." She quickly pressed the red hang-up button. Somehow, she knew there was no way she could leave the shelter of her little condo in the middle of nowhere, or the safety of the deep cave at the hospital with handsome scanner voice, or the purity of overhead paging a Code Blue, thinking maybe you helped someone survive.

"I love you," she said to Freddie, "and you," to Dr. Crusher, "and you," she kissed Higgs-Boson's tiny wet nose. "You are beloved."

Things were good. Juliet trusted in stuff and it seemed to be working for her. She had learned a lot and met some fabulous people.

"Glo?"

"Hey, sister."

"Hey."

"I'm all over it."

"See you tomorrow?"

"You got it."

"Bye."

"Hey. Lay off the wine."

"Okay, bye."

"Bye."

Sabine grabbed her remote and turned on the small television by the foot of the bed.

Jon Mundy's *Miracles in Manhattan* channel was on her YouTube, and he was reading from Chapter 27,

saying, "You are the dreamer of the world of dreams…
" . She flashed back on 1979 when she attended *A Course in Miracles* lectures at the 92nd Street Y. And now, Jon Mundy, a boomer like herself, was almost as attractive as the handsome scanner voice. If she ever got back to New York, she would attend one of his lectures.

Fellini's *8 ½* was on her *Watch Next* list. She tapped it on. She thought of Juliet. She thought of *Dr. Strangelove*. She thought of Freya, the beautiful, long-haired family cat when she was seven, and wondered whatever became of her. She thought of Copacabana Beach and the warmth of that Brazilian summer night, the smell of cooking coming from the restaurants, the lights from Rio in the background, the delight she and Jean-Paul shared in the magical lizard with the orchid in its mouth. Life was rich. It was good.

Freddie Mercury was still pummeling the quilt on the bed, his claws going in and out, his loud purring and unblinking gaze demanding Sabine's attention. She hugged him and reached to the bottom shelf of the nightstand for *Flow: The Psychology of Optimal Experience* by Mihaly Csikszentmihalyl. For no reason at all, she trusted that this book she found in the sale bin at the Walmart would reveal the missing intel that she needed. You never knew when something might work out.

At 4am her phone alarm woke her and the kitties with her Global Cocktail Chilled station playing *Jazz Juice: Sound of the Summer 52nd Street*. She smiled, stretched her arms over her head, and then hugged each kitty in turn.

"Thank you for calling Trummel Hospital, how may I help you this morning?" Sabine waved goodbye and a thank you to Valentine, who had pointed out a wrong extension number on the day's emergency surgical on-call list.

"I need help. I'm out of breath."

"Okay, hold on, I'll transfer you to the ER."

"No! I don't want the ER."

"Do you want to call 911?"

"No! I need help."

"Okay, dear, no problem, I'm transferring you to a Help Specialist. She may answer the phone 'ER,' but that's only because that's where she's sitting. Okay?"

"Okay."

"Okay then."

Made in the USA
Middletown, DE
15 December 2019